THE BRIGHT SHAWL

THE
BRIGHT SHAWL

JOSEPH HERGESHEIMER

NEW YORK
ALFRED·A·KNOPF
1922

COPYRIGHT, 1922, BY
ALFRED A. KNOPF, Inc.

Published, October, 1922

Second Printing, October, 1922
Third Printing, October, 1922

Set up and electrotyped by the Vail-Ballou Co., Binghamton. N. Y.
Paper furnished by W. F. Etherington & Co., New York, N. Y.
Printed and bound by the Plimpton Press, Norwood, Mass.

MANUFACTURED IN THE UNITED STATES OF AMERICA

For

Hamilton and Phœbe Gilkyson junior

in their fine drawing-room

at Mont Clare

THE BRIGHT SHAWL

WHEN Howard Gage had gone, his mother's brother sat with his head bowed in frowning thought. The frown, however, was one of perplexity rather than disapproval: he was wholly unable to comprehend the younger man's attitude toward his experiences in the late war. The truth was, Charles Abbott acknowledged, that he understood nothing, nothing at all, about the present young. Indeed, if it hadn't been for the thoroughly absurd, the witless, things they constantly did, dispensing with their actual years he would have considered them the present aged. They were so—well, so gloomy.

Yet, in view of the gaiety of the current parties, the amounts of gin consumed, it wasn't precisely gloom that enveloped them. Charles Abbott searched his mind for a definition, for light on a subject dark to a degree beyond any mere figure of speech. Yes, darkness particularly described Howard. The satirical bitterness of

[9]

his references to the "glorious victory in France" was actually a little unbalanced. The impression Abbott had received was of bestiality choked in mud. His nephew was amazingly clear, vivid and logical, in his memories and opinions; they couldn't, as he stated them in a kind of frozen fury, be easily controverted.

What, above everything else, appeared to dominate Howard Gage was a passion for reality, for truth—all the unequivocal facts—in opposition to a conventional or idealized statement. Particularly, he regarded the slightest sentiment with a suspicion that reached hatred. Abbott's thoughts centered about the word idealized; there, he told himself, a ray of perception might be cast into Howard's obscurity; since the most evident fact of all was that he cherished no ideals, no sustaining vision of an ultimate dignity behind men's lives.

The boy, for example, was without patriotism; or, at least, he hadn't a trace of the emotional loyalty that had fired the youth of Abbott's day. There was nothing sacrificial in Howard Gage's conception of life and duty, no allegiance outside his immediate need. Selfish, Charles Abbott decided. What upset him was the other's coldness: damn it, a young man had no business to be so literal! Youth was a time for generous transforming passions, for heroics. The qualities of absolute justice and consistency should come only with increasing age—the inconsiderable compensations for the other ability to be rapt in uncritical enthusiasms.

Charles Abbott sighed and raised his head. He was sitting in the formal narrow reception room of his city house. The street outside was narrow, too; it ran for only a square, an old thoroughfare with old brick houses, once no more than a service alley for the larger dwellings back of which it ran. Now, perfectly retaining its quietude, it had acquired a new dignity of residence: because of its favorable, its exclusive, situation, it was occupied by young married people of highly desirable connections. Abbott, well past sixty and single, was the only person there of his age and condition.

October was advanced and, though it was hardly past four in the afternoon, the golden sunlight falling the length of the street was already darkling with the faded day. A warm glow enveloped the brick façades and the window panes of aged, faintly iridescent glass; there was a remote sound of automobile horns, the illusive murmur of a city never, at its loudest, loud; and,

[11]

through the walls, the notes of a piano, charming and melancholy.

After a little he could distinguish the air—it was Liszt's Spanish Rhapsody. The accent of its measure, the jota, was at once perceptible and immaterial; and overwhelmingly, through its magic of suggestion, a blinding vision of his own youth—so different from Howard's—swept over Charles Abbott. It was exactly as though, again twenty-three, he were standing in the incandescent sunlight of Havana; in, to be precise, the Parque Isabel. This happened so suddenly, so surprisingly, that it oppressed his heart; he breathed with a sharpness which resembled a gasp; the actuality around him was blurred as though his eyes were slightly dazzled.

The playing continued intermittently, while its power to stir him grew in an overwhelming volume. He had had no idea that he was still capable of such profound feeling, such emotion spun, apparently, from the tunes only potent with the young. He was confused—even, alone, embarrassed—at the tightness of his throat, and made a decided effort to regain a reasonable mind. He turned again to the consideration of Howard Gage, of his lack of ideals; and,

[12]

still in the flood of the re-created past, he saw, in the difference between Howard and the boy in Havana, what, for himself anyhow, was the trouble with the present.

Yes, his premonition had been right—the youth of today were without the high and romantic causes the service of which had so brightly colored his own early years. Not patriotism alone but love had suffered; and friendship, he was certain, had all but disappeared; such friendship as had bound him to Andrés Escobar. Andrés! Charles Abbott hadn't thought of him consciously for months. Now, with the refrain of the piano, the jota, running through his thoughts, Andrés was as real as he had been forty years ago.

It was forty years almost to the month since they had gone to the public ball, the danzón, in the Tacon Theatre. That, however, was at the close of the period which had recurred to him like a flare in the dusk of the past. After the danzón the blaze of his sheer fervency had been reduced, cooled, to maturity. But not, even in the peculiarly brutal circumstances of his transition, sharply; only now Charles Abbott definitely realized that he had left in Cuba, lost there,

[13]

THE BRIGHT SHAWL

the illusions which were synonymous with his young intensity.

After that nothing much had absorbed him, very little had happened. In comparison with the spectacular brilliancy of his beginning, the remainder of life had seemed level if not actually drab. Certainly the land to which he had returned was dull against the vivid south, the tropics. But he couldn't go back to Havana, he had felt, even after the Spanish Government was expelled, any more than he could find in the Plaza de Armas his own earlier self. The whole desirable affair had been one—the figures of his loves and detestations, the paseos and glorietas and parques of the city, now, he had heard, so changed, formed a unity destroyed by the missing of any single element.

He wasn't, though, specially considering himself, but rather the sustaining beliefs that so clearly marked the divergence between Howard's day and his own. This discovery, he felt, was of deep importance, it explained so much that was apparently inexplicable. Charles Abbott asserted silently, dogmatically, that a failure of spirit had occurred . . . there was no longer such supreme honor as Andrés Escobar's. The dance measure in the Spanish Rhapsody grew louder

[14]

and more insistent, and through it he heard the
castanets of La Clavel, he saw the superb flame
of her body in the brutal magnificence of the
fringed mantón like Andalusia incarnate.

*

* *

He had a vision of the shawl itself, and, once
more, seemed to feel the smooth dragging heavi-
ness of its embroidery. The burning square of
its colors unfolded before him, the incredible ma-
gentas, the night blues and oranges and emerald
and vermilion, worked into broad peonies and
roses wreathed in leaves. And suddenly he felt
again that, not only prefiguring Spain, it was
symbolical of the youth, the time, that had gone.
Thus the past appeared to him, wrapped bright
and precious in the shawl of memory.

No woman that Howard Gage might dream of
could have worn La Clavel's mantón; it would
have consumed her like a breath of fire, leaving
a white ash hardly more than distinguishable
from the present living actuality. Women cast
up a prodigious amount of smoke now, a most
noisy crackling, but Charles Abbott doubted the
blaze within them. Water had been thrown on
it. Their grace, too, the dancing about which

[15]

they made such a stir,—not to compare it with La Clavel's but with no better than Pilar's—was hardly more than a rapid clumsy posturing. Where was the young man now who could dance for two hours without stopping on a spot scarcely bigger than the rim of his silk hat?

Where, indeed, was the silk hat!

Even men's clothes had suffered in the common decline: black satin and gold, nicely cut trousers, the propriety of pumps, had all vanished. Charles Abbott recalled distinctly the care with which he had assembled the clothing to be taken to Cuba, the formal dress of evening, with a plum-colored cape, and informal linens for the tropical days. The shirt-maker had filled his box with the finest procurable cambrics and tallest stocks. Trivialities, yet they indicated what had once been breeding; but now, incredibly, that was regarded as trivial.

The Spanish Rhapsody had ceased, and the sun was all but withdrawn from the street; twilight was gathering, particularly in Charles Abbott's reception room. The gilded eagle of the old American clock on the over-mantel seemed almost to flutter its carved wings, the fragile rose mahogany spinet held what light there was, but the pair of small brocaded sofas had lost their

severe definition. Charles Abbott's emotion, as
well, subsided, its place taken by a concentrated
effort to put together the details of a scene which
had assumed, in his perplexity about Howard, a
present significance.

He heard, with a momentarily diverted attention, the closing of the front door beyond,
women's voices on the pavement and the changing gears of a motor: Mrs. Vauxn and her
daughter were going out early for dinner.
They lived together—the girl had married into
the navy—and it was the former who played the
piano. The street, after their departure, was
silent again. How different it was from the
clamorous gaiety of Havana.

Not actual sickness, Charles Abbott proceeded,
but the delicacy of his lungs, following scarlet
fever, had taken him south. A banking asso-
ciate of his father's, recommending Cuba, had,
at the same time, pointedly qualified his suggestion; and this secondary consideration had determined Charles on Havana. The banker had
added that Cuba was the most healthful place
he knew for anyone with no political attach-
ments. There political activity, more than an indiscretion, was fatal. What did he mean?
Charles Abbott had asked; and the other had

replied with a single ominous word, Spain.

There was, it was brought out, a growing and potent, but secretive, spirit of rebellion against the Government, to which Seville was retaliating with the utmost open violence. This was spread not so much through the people, the country, at large, as it was concentrated in the cities, in Santiago de Cuba and Havana; and there it was practically limited to the younger members of aristocratic families. Every week boys—they were no more for all their sounding pronunciamientos—were being murdered in the fosses of Cabañas fortress. Women of the greatest delicacy, suspected of sympathy with nationalistic ideals, were thrown into the filthy pens of town prostitutes. Everywhere a limitless system of espionage was combating the gathering of circles, tertulias, for the planning of a Cuba liberated from a bloody and intolerable tyranny.

Were these men, Charles pressed his query, really as young as himself? Younger, some of them, by five and six years. And they were shot by a file of soldiers' muskets? Eight students at the university had been executed at once for a disproved charge that they had scrawled an insulting phrase on the glass

[18]

THE BRIGHT SHAWL

door of the tomb of a Cuban Volunteer. At
this the elder Abbott had looked so dubious that
Charles hastily abandoned his questioning.
Enough of that sort of thing had been shown; already his mother was unalterably opposed to
Cuba; and there he intended at any price to go.
But those tragedies and reprisals, the champion
of his determination insisted, were limited, as he
had begun by saying, to the politically involved.
No more engaging or safer city than Havana existed for the delight of young travelling Americans with an equal amount of money and good
sense. He had proceeded to indicate the temper-
ate pleasures of Havana; but, then, Charles Abbott had no ear for sensuous enjoyment. His
mind was filled by the other vision of heroic
youth dying for the ideal of liberty.

He had never before given Cuba, under Spanish rule, a thought; but at a chance sentence it
dominated him completely; all his being had
been tinder for the spark of its romantic
spirit. This, naturally, he had carefully concealed from his parents, for, during the days that
immediately followed, Cuba as a possibility was
continuously argued. Soon his father, basing
his decision on Charles' gravity of character,
was in favor of the change; and in the end his

[19]

mother, at whose prescience he wondered, was
overborne.

Well, he was for Havana! His cabin on the
Morro Castle was secured, that notable trunkful
of personal effects packed; and his father, greatly
to Charles' surprise, outside all women's knowledge, gave him a small derringer with a handle
of mother-of-pearl. He was, now, the elder told
him, almost a man; and, while it was inconceivable that he would have a use for the pistol, he
must accustom himself to such responsibility.
He wouldn't need it; but if he did, there, with its
greased cartridges in their short ugly chambers,
it was. "Never shoot in a passion," the excellent advice went on; "only a cool hand is steady,
and remember that it hasn't much range." It
was for desperate necessity at a very short distance.

With the derringer lying newly in his grasp, his
eyes steadily on his father's slightly anxious gaze,
Charles asseverated that he would faithfully attend every instruction. At the identical moment
of this commitment he pictured himself firing
into the braided tunic of a beastly Spanish officer and supporting a youthful Cuban patriot,
dying pallidly of wounds, in his free arm. The
Morro Castle hadn't left its New York dock be-

fore he had determined just what part he would take in the liberation of Cuba—he'd lead a hopeless demonstration in the center of Havana, at the hour when the city was its brightest and the band playing most gaily; his voice, sharp like a shot, so soon to be stilled in death, would stop the insolence of music.

*

*　　　　　　*

This was not a tableau of self-glorification or irresponsible youth, he proceeded; it was more significant than a spirit of adventure. His determination rested on the abstraction of liberty for an oppressed people; he saw Cuba as a place which, after great travail, would become the haunt of perfect peace. That, Charles felt, was not only a possibility but inevitable; he saw the forces of life drawn up in such a manner—the good on one side facing the bad on the other. There was no mingling of the ranks, no grey; simply, conveniently, black and white. And, in the end, the white would completely triumph; it would be victorious for the reason that heaven must reign over hell. God was supreme.

Charles wasn't at all religious, he came of a blood which delegated to its women the rites and

[21]

responsibilities of the church; but there was no question in his mind, no doubt, of the Protestant theological map; augustness lay concretely behind the sky; hell was no mere mediæval fantasy. He might ignore this in daily practice, yet it held him within its potent if invisible barriers. Charles Abbott believed it. The supremacy of God, suspended above the wickedness of Spain, would descend and crush it.

Ranged, therefore, squarely on the side of the angels, mentally he swept forward in confidence, sustained by the glitter of their invincible pinions. The spending of his life, he thought, was a necessary part of the consummation; somehow without that his vision lost radiance. A great price would be required, but the result—eternal happiness on that island to which he was taking linen suits in winter! Charles had a subconscious conception of the heroic doctrine of the destruction of the body for the soul's salvation.

The Morro Castle, entering a wind like the slashing of a stupendous dull grey sword, slowly and uncomfortably steamed along her course. Most of the passengers at once were seasick, and either retired or collapsed in a leaden row under the lee of the deck cabins. But this indisposition didn't touch Charles, and it pleased his sense

THE BRIGHT SHAWL

of dignity. He appeared, erect and capable, at
breakfast, and through the morning promenaded
the unsteady deck. He attended the gambling
in the smoking saloon, and listened gravely
to the fragmentary hymns attempted on Sunday.

These human activities were all definitely outside him; charged with a higher purpose, he
watched them comprehendingly, his lips bearing
the shadow of a saddened smile; essentially he
was alone, isolated. Or at least he was at the
beginning of the four days' journey—he kept col-
liding with the rotund figure of a man wrapped
to the eyes in a heavy cloak until, finally, from
progressing in opposite directions, they fell
into step together. To Charles' delight, the
other was a Cuban, Domingo Escobar, who lived
in Havana, on the Prado.

Charles Abbott learned this from the flourish-
ing card given in return for his own. Escobar
he found to be a man with a pleasant and considerate disposition; indeed, he maintained a scru-
pulous courtesy toward Charles far transcending
any he would have had, from a man so much
older, at home. Domingo Escobar, it developed,
had a grown son, Vincente, twenty-eight years
old; a boy perhaps Charles' own age—no, Andrés

would be two, three, years younger; and Narcisa.
The latter, his daughter, Escobar, unashamed,
described as a budding white rose.

Charles wasn't interested in that, his thoughts
were definitely turned from girls, however flow-
erlike; but he was engaged by Vincente and Andrés. He asked a great many questions about
them, all tending to discover, if possible, the activity of their patriotism. This, though, was a
subject which Domingo Escobar resolutely ignored.

Once, when Charles put a direct query with
relation to Spain in Cuba, the older man,
abruptly replying at a tangent, ignored his question. It would be necessary to ask Andrés
Escobar himself. That he would have an opportunity to do this was assured, for Andrés'
parent, who knew the Abbotts' banking friend
intimately, had told Charles with flattering sin-
cerity how welcome he would be at the Escobar
dwelling on the Prado.

The Prado, it began to be clear, of all the
possible places of residence in Havana, was the
best; the Escobars went to Paris when they
willed; and, altogether, Charles told himself, he
had made a very fortunate beginning. He
picked up, from various sources on the steamer,

useful tags of knowledge about his destination:

The Inglaterra, to which he had been directed, was a capital hotel, but outside the walls. Still, the Calle del Prado, the Paseo there, were quite gay; and before them was the sweep of the Parque Isabel, where the band played. At the Hotel St. Louis, next door, many of the Spanish officers had their rooms, but at the hour of dinner they gathered in the Café Dominica. The Noble Havana was celebrated for its camarones —shrimps, Charles learned—and the Tuileries, at the juncture of Consulado and San Rafael Streets, had a salon upstairs especially for women. Most of his dinners, however, he would get at the Restaurant Français, excellently kept by François Garçon on Cuba Street, number seventy-two.

There he would encounter the majority of his young fellow countrymen in Havana; the Café El Louvre would serve for sherbets after the theatre, and the Aguila de Oro. . . . The Plaza de Toros, of course, he would frequent: it was on Belascoin Street near the sea. The afternoon fights only were fashionable; the bulls killed in the morning were no more than toro del aguadiente. And the cockpit was at the Valla de Gallo.

[25]

There were other suggestions as well, put mostly in the form of ribald inquiry; but toward them Charles Abbott persisted in an attitude of uncommunicative disdain. His mind, his whole determination, had been singularly purified; he had a sensation of remoteness from the flesh; his purpose killed earthly desire. He thought of himself now as dedicated to that: Charles reviewed the comfortable amount of his letter of credit, his personal qualifications, the derringer mounted in mother-of-pearl, in the light of one end. It annoyed him that he couldn't, at once, plunge into this with Domingo Escobar; but, whenever he approached that ordinarily responsive gentleman with anything political, he grew morose and silent, or else, more maddening still, deliberately put Charles' interest aside. The derringer, however, brought out an unexpected and gratifying stir.

Escobar had stopped in Charles' cabin, and the latter, with a studied air of the casual, displayed the weapon on his berth. "You must throw it away," Escobar exclaimed dramatically; "at once, now, through the porthole."

"I can't do that," Charles explained; "it was a gift from my father; besides, I'm old enough for such things."

[26]

"A gift from your father, perhaps," the other echoed; "but did he tell you, I wonder, how you were going to get it into Cuba? Did he explain what the Spanish officials would do if they found you with a pistol? Dama de Caridad, do you suppose Cuba is New York! The best you could hope for would be deportation. Into the sea with it."

But this Charles Abbott refused to do, though he would, he agreed, conceal it beyond the ingenuity of Spain; and Escobar left him in a muttering anger. Charles felt decidedly encouraged: a palpable degree of excitement, of tense anticipation, had been granted him.

*

*   *

Yet his first actual breath of the tropics, of Cuba, was very different, charged and surcharged with magical peace: the steamer was enveloped in an evening of ineffable lovely blueness. The sun faded from the world of water and left an ultramarine undulating flood with depths of clear black, the sky was a tender gauze of color which, as night approached, was sewn with a glimmer that became curiously apparent, seemingly nearby, stars. The air that brushed

[27]

Charles' cheek was slow and warm; its warmth was fuller, heavier with potency, than any summer he had known. Accelerating his imagination it dissipated his energies; he lounged supine in his chair, long past midnight, lulled by the slight rise and fall of the sea, gathered up benignly into the beauty above him.

Later he had to stir himself into the energy of packing, for the Morro Castle was docking early in the morning. He closed his bag thoughtfully, the derringer on a shelf. Escobar had spoken about it, warning him, again; and it was apparent that no obvious place of concealment would be sufficient. At last he hit on an excellent expedient—he would suspend it inside the leg of a trouser. He fell asleep, still saturated with the placid blue immensity without, and woke sharply, while it was still dark. But it was past four, and he rose and dressed. The deck was empty, deserted, and the light in the pilot house showed a solitary intent countenance under a glazed visor. There was, of course, no sign of Cuba.

A wind freshened, it blew steadily with no change of temperature, like none of the winds with which he was familiar. It appeared to blow the night away, astern. The caged light grew dull, there were rifts in the darkness, gleams over the tranquil sea, and the morning opened like a flower sparkling in dew. The limitless reach of the water flashed in silver planes; miniature rainbows cascaded in the spray at the steamer's bow; a flight of sailing fish skittered by the side. Far ahead there was a faint silhouette, like the print of a tenuous green-grey cloud, on the sea. It grew darker, bolder; and Charles Abbott realized that it was an island.

Cuba came rapidly nearer; he could see now that it wasn't pale; its foliage was heavy, glossy, almost sombre. The Morro Castle bore to the left, but he was unable to make out an opening, a possible city, on the coast. The water regained its intense blue, at once transparent, clear, and dyed with pigment. The other travellers were all on deck: Charles moved toward Domingo Escobar, but he eluded him. Undoubtedly Escobar had the conjunction of the derringer and the Spanish customs in mind. A general uneasiness permeated the small throng; they conversed with a forced triviality, or, sunk in thought, said nothing.

Then, with the sudden drama of a crash of brass, of an abruptly lifting curtain, they swung into Havana harbor. Charles was simulta-

[29]

neously amazed at a great many things—the narrowness of the entrance, the crowded ships in what was no more than a rift of the sea, a long pink fortress above ·him at the left, and the city, Havana itself, immediately before him. His utmost desire was satisfied by that first glimpse. Why, he cried mentally, hadn't he been told that it was a city of white marble? That was the impression it gave him—a miraculous whiteness, a dream city, crowning the shining blue tide.

Every house was hung with balconies on long shuttered windows, and everywhere were parks and palms, tall palms with smooth pewter-like trunks and short palms profusely leaved. Here, then, white and green, was the place of his dedication; he was a little dashed at its size and vigor and brilliancy.

The steamer was scarcely moving when the customs officials came on board; and, as the drift ceased, a swarm of boats like scows with·awnings aft clustered about them. Hotel runners clambered up the sides, and in an instant there was a pandemonium of Spanish and disjointed English. A man whose cap bore the sign Hotel Telégrafo clutched Charles Abbott's arm, but he sharply drew away, repeating the single word, "Inglaterra!" The porter of that hotel soon

[30]

discovered him, and, with a fixed reassuring smile, got together all the baggage for his guests.

Charles, instructed by Domingo Escobar, ignored the demand for passports, and proceeded to the boat indicated as the Inglaterra's. It was piled with luggage, practically awash; yet the boatmen urged it ashore, to the custom house, in a mad racing with the whole churning flotilla. The rigor of the landing examination, Charles thought impatiently, had been ridiculously exaggerated; but, stepping into a hack, two men in finely striped linen, carrying canes with green tassels, peremptorily stopped him. Charles was unable to grasp the intent of their rapid Spanish, when one ran his hands dexterously over his body. He explored the pockets, tapped Charles' back, and then drew aside. When, at last, he was seated in the hack, the position of the derringer was awkward, and carefully he shifted it.

An intimate view of Havana increased rather than diminished its evident charms. The heat, Charles found, though extreme, was less oppressive than the dazzling light; the sun blazing on white walls, on walls of primrose and cobalt, in the wide verdant openings, positively blinded him. He passed narrow streets over which awnings were hung from house to house, statues, fountains, a broad way with files of unfamiliar trees, and stopped with a clatter before the Inglaterra.

It faced on a broad covered pavement, an arcade, along which, farther down, were companies of small iron tables and chairs; and it was so foreign to Charles, so fascinating, that he stood lost in gazing. A hotel servant in white, at his elbow, recalled the necessity of immediate arrangements, and he went on into a high cool corridor set with a marble flooring. At the office he exchanged his passport for a solemn printed warning and interminable succession of directions; and then, climbing an impressive stair, he was ushered into a room where the ceiling was so far above him that once more he was overcome by strangeness and surprise.

He unpacked slowly, with a gratifying sense of the mature significance of his every gesture; and, in the stone tub hidden by a curtain in a corner, had a refreshing bath. There was a single window rising from the tiled floor eight or ten feet, and he opened double shutters, discovering a shallow iron-railed balcony. Before him was a squat yellow building with a wide complicated façade; it reached back for a square, and Charles decided that it was the Tacon Theatre.

On the left was the Parque de Isabel, with its grass plots and gravel walks, its trees and iron settees, gathered about the statue of Isabel II.

Charles Abbott's confidence left him little by little; what had seemed so easy in New York, so apparent, was uncertain with Havana about him. The careless insolence of the inspectors with the green-tasseled canes at once filled him with indignation and depression. How was he to begin his mission? Without a word of Spanish he couldn't even make it known. There was Andrés Escobar to consider: his father had told Charles that he knew a few words of English. Meanwhile, hungry, he went down to the eleven o'clock breakfast.

*

*   *

A ceremonious head waiter led him to a small table by a long window on the Parque, where, gazing hastily at the breakfasts around him, he managed, with the assistance of his waiter's limited English, to repeat their principal features. These were fruit and salads, coffee flavored with salt, and French bread. Clear white curtains swung at the window in a barely perceptible current of air, and he had glimpses of the

[33]

expanse without, now veiled and now intolerably brilliant. His dissatisfaction, doubts, vanished in an extraordinary sense of well-being, or settled importance and elegance. There were many people in the dining-room, it was filled with the unfamiliar sound of Spanish; the men, dark, bearded and brilliant-eyed, in white linens, with their excitable hands, specially engaged his attention, for it was to them he was addressed.

The women he glanced over with a detached and indulgent manner: they were, on the whole, a little fatter than necessary; but their voices were soft and their dress and jewels, even so early in the day, nicely elaborate. All his interest was directed to the Cubans present; other travellers, like—or, rather, unlike—himself, Americans, French and English, planning in their loud several tongues the day's excursions, or breakfasting with gazes fastened on Hingray's English and Spanish Conversations, Charles carefully ignored.

He felt, because of the depth of his own implication, his passionate self-commitment, here, infinitely superior to more casual, to blinder, journeyings. He disliked the English arrogance, the American clothes, and the suspicious parsimony of the French. Outside, in the main corridor of the hotel, he paused undecided; practically no one, he saw, in the Parque Isabel, was walking; there was an unending broad stream of single horse victorias for hire; but he couldn't ask any driver he saw to conduct him to the heart of the Cuban party of liberty.

The strongest of all his recognitions was the fact that he had no desire—but a marked distaste —for sightseeing; he didn't want to be identified, in the eyes of Havana, with the circulating throng of the superficially curious. In the end he strolled away from the Inglaterra, to the left, and discovered the Prado. It was a wide avenue with the promenade in the center shaded by rows of trees with small burnished leaves. There, he remembered, was where the Escobars lived, and he wondered which of the imposing dwellings, blue or white, with sweeping pillars and carved balconies and great iron-bound doors, was theirs. He passed a fencing school and gymnasium; a dilapidated theatre of wood pasted with old French playbills; fountains with lions' heads; and came to the sea. It reached in an idyllic and unstirred blue away to the flawless horizon, with, on the rocks of its shore, a company of parti-colored bath-houses. There was an old fort, a gate—which, he could see, once formed

[35]

part of the city wall—bearing on its top a row of rusted and antiquated cannon. Slopes of earth led down from the battery, and beyond he entered a covered stone way with a parapet dropping to the tranquil tide. After an open space, the Maestranza, he came to a pretty walk; it was the Paseo de Valdez, with trees, stone seats and a rippling breeze.

Charles Abbott indolently examined an arch, fallen into disrepair, erected, its tablet informed him, by the corps of Royal Engineers. He sat on a bench, saturated by the hot vivid peace; before him reached the narrow entrance of the bay with, on the farther hand, the long pink wall of the Cabañas. A drift of military music came to him from the fortress. . . . A great love for Havana stirred in his heart; already, after only a few hours, he was familiar, contented, there. It seemed to Charles that he understood its spirit; the beauty of palms and marble was what, in the bleak north, all his life he had longed for. The constriction of his breathing had vanished.

The necessity for an immediate and violent action had lessened; he would, when the time came, act; he was practically unlimited in days and money. Charles decided, however, to begin at once the study of Spanish; and he'd arrange for lessons at the Fencing School. Both of those accomplishments were imperative to his final intention. He lingered on the beach without an inclination to move—he had been lower physically than he realized. The heat increased, the breeze and band stopped, and finally he rose and returned to the Inglaterra. There the high cool shadow of his room was so soothing that he fell into a sound slumber and was waked only by a pounding at his door past the middle of afternoon.

A servant tendered him a card that bore engraved the name Andrés Escobar. He would see Mr. Escobar, he sent word, as soon as he could be dressed. And, choosing his garb in a mingling of haste and particular care, he was permeated by an indefinable excitement. Facing Andrés, he had a sensation of his own clumsiness, his inept attitude; for the other, younger than he in appearance, was faultless in bearing: in immaculately ironed linen, a lavender tie and sprig of mimosa, he was an impressive figure of the best fashion. But Andrés Escobar was far more than that: his sensitive delicately modelled dark face, the clear brown eyes and level lips, were stamped with a superfine personality.

His English, as his father had said, was halting, confined to the merest formal phrases, but his tones were warm with hospitality.

"It was polite of you to come so soon," Charles replied; "and your father was splendid to me on the steamer."

"How do you like Havana?" Andrés asked.

"I love it!" Charles Abbott exclaimed, in a burst of enthusiasm, but of which, immediately after, he was ashamed. "I was thinking this morning," he continued more stiffly, "when I had hardly got here, how much at home I felt. That's funny, too; for it's entirely different from all I have known."

"You like it!" Andrés Escobar reflected his unreserved tone. "That's good; I am very, very glad. You must come to our house, Papa sends you this." He smiled delightfully.

They were standing, and Charles waved toward the dining-room. "Suppose we go in there and have a drink." In Havana he continually found himself in situations of the most gratifying maturity—here he was, in the dining-room of the Inglaterra Hotel, with a tall rum punch before him, and a mature looking cigar. He was a little doubtful about the latter, its length was formidable; and he delayed lighting it until Andrés had partly eclipsed himself in smoke. But, to

[38]

his private satisfaction, Charles enjoyed the cigar completely.

He liked his companion enormously, noticing, as they sat in a comfortable silence, fresh details: Andrés' hair, ink-black, grew in a peak on his forehead; the silk case which held his cigars was bound in gold; his narrow shoes were patent leather with high heels. But what, above all else, impressed Charles, was his evidently worldly poise, the palpable air of experience that clung to him. Andrés was at once younger and much older than himself.

"How are you interested?" Andrés asked, "in . . . girls? I know some very nice ones."

"Not in the least," Charles Abbott replied decidedly; "the only thing I care for is politics and the cause of justice and freedom."

*

*   *

Andrés Escobar gazed swiftly at the occupied tables around them; not far away there was a party of Spanish officers in loose short tunics and blue trousers. Then, without commenting on Charles' assertion, he drank from his glass of punch. "Some very nice girls," he repeated. Charles was overwhelmed with chagrin at his indiscretion; Andrés would think that he was a babbling idiot. At the same time he was slightly impatient: his faith in the dangers of Havana had been shaken by the city's aspect of profound placidity, its air of unalloyed pleasure. "You should know my friends," Andrés went on conversationally; "Remigio Florez, they are great coffee planters, and Jaime—Jaime Quintara —and Tirso Labrador. They will welcome you, as I."

Charles explained his intention of learning Spanish, of fencing; and the other promised his unreserved assistance. He would have a teacher of languages sent to the hotel and himself take Charles to the Fencing School. "Tomorrow," he promised. The drinks were finished, the cigars consumed in long ashes, and Andrés Escobar rose to go. As they walked toward the Paseo the Cuban said, "You must be very careful, liberty is a dangerous word; it is discussed only in private; in our tertulia you may speak." He held out a straight forward palm. "We shall be friends."

Again in his room, Charles dwelt on Andrés, conscious of the birth of a great liking, the friendship the other had put into words. He wanted to be like Andrés, as slender and grace-

ful, with his hair in a peak and a worldly, con-
tained manner. Charles was thin, rather than
slender, more awkward than not; decidedly fragile in appearance. And his experience of life
had been less than nothing. Yet he would make
up for this lack by the fervor of his attachment
to the cause of Cuba. He recalled all the stories
he knew of foreign soldiers heroic in an adopted
cause; that was an even more ideal form of service than the natural attachment to a land of
birth.

He moved a chair out on his balcony, and
sat above the extended irregular roof of the
Tacon Theatre, watching the dusk flood the
white marble ways. The lengthening shadows of
the Parque blurred, joined in one; the façades
were golden and then dimly violet; the Gate of
Montserrat lost its boldness of outline. Cries
rose from the streets, "Cuidado! Cuidado!" and
"Narranjas, narranjas dulces." The evening
news sheets were called in long falling inflections.

What surprised him was that, although he had
more than an ordinary affection for his home,
his father and mother, now, here, they were of
no importance, no reality, to him. He never,
except by an objective effort, gave the north, the
past, a thought. He was carried above personal

[41]

relationships and familiar regard; at a blow his old ties had been severed; the new held him in the grip of their infinite possibilities. All the petty things of self were obscured in the same way that the individual aspects of the city below him were being merged into one dignity of tone.

Yet, at the same time, his mood had a charming reality—the suaveness of Andrés Escobar. His, Charles Abbott's, would be a select, an aristocratic, fate; the end, when it overtook him, would find him in beautiful snowy linens, dignified, exclusive, to the last. His would be no pot-house brawling. That was his double necessity, the highest form of good in circumstances of the first breeding. One, perhaps, to his æsthetic fibre, was as important as the other. And, dressing for dinner, he spoiled three shirts in the exact right fixing of his studs.

In the dining-room, he pressed a liberal sum of American money on the head waiter, and was conducted to the table he had occupied at breakfast. Everyone, practically, except some unspeakable tourists, was in formal clothes; and the conversations, the sparkling light, were like the champagne everywhere evident. Charles chose a Spanish wine, the Marquis de Riscal; and prolonged his sitting over coffee and a cigar, a Partagas, like those in Andrés' silk case. He had never before tasted coffee with such a rich thick savor, its fragrance alone, blending with the blue smoke of his cigar, filled him with pleasure.

The room was long, tiled, and had, against the far wall, a great mirror which held in reverse the gay sweep of the tables, the heavily powdered shoulders of women, the prismatic flashes of diamonds and men's animated faces. The reflections were almost as fascinating as the reality, and Charles gazed from one to the other.

Drinking, he saw, was universal, but none of the Cubans were drunk; and for that reason his attention was held by two men at the table next to his: the waiter had left a bottle of brandy, and the individual facing Charles, with a sallow face from which depended, like a curtain, a square-cut black beard, was filling and refilling his thimble-sized glass. He was watching, with a shifting intentness of gaze, all who entered; and suddenly, as Charles' eyes were on him, he put down his half-lifted brandy and a hand went under the fold of his coat.

Charles turned, involuntarily, and saw a small immaculate Cuban with grey hair and a ribband in his buttonhole advancing among the tables. He was a man of distinguished appear-

[43]

ance, important it was evident, for a marked number of people bowed as he passed. When he had gone on, the bearded individual rose, swaying slightly, and, with his hand still in his coat rapidly overtook the other.

Charles Abbott had an impulse to cry out; but, oppressed by a sense of helpless dread, impending disaster, without a sound or power of movement he followed the course of the second figure. The two were now at the end of the dining-room, close to the mirror, when the man with the decoration stopped and turned sharply. There was the sudden stabbing report of a pistol, and, immediately following, a loud splintering crash. Charles had the crazy illusion that a man who had been shot was made of china, and would be found in broken bits on the floor.

There was an instantaneous hysterical uproar, dominated by the screams of women; in the panic which rose there was a rush for the entrance, a swirl of tearing satin and black dress coats. Then, even before he heard the concerted derisive amazement, Charles realized that, dazed by the brandy, the intended murderer had fired at the reflection of his mark in the glass.

What an utterly ridiculous error; and yet his hands were wet and cold, his heart pounding.

THE BRIGHT SHAWL

Something of the masking gaiety, the appearance of innocent high spirits, was stripped from the dining-room of the Inglaterra, from Havana. There was an imperative need for Andrés Escobar's caution. Charles' equanimity returned: with a steady hand he poured out more coffee. He was ashamed of his emotion; but, by heaven, that was the first of such violence he had witnessed; he knew that it happened, to a large degree its possibility had brought him to Cuba; yet directly before him, in a square beard and a decorating ribband! . . . On the floor were the torn painted gauze and broken ivory sticks of a woman's fan.

*

* *

The echo of that futile shot followed Charles Abbott to the Escobars', where, because of the often repeated names of its principals, he recognized that the affair was being minutely discussed. The room in which they sat was octagonal, with the high panels of its walls no more than frames for towering glass doors set in dark wood; above were serrated openings, Eastern in form, and the doors were supported by paired columns of glacial white marble. It was entered through a long corridor of pillars capped

[45]

in black onyx with wicker chairs, a tiling laid in arabesques and potted palms; and opposite was the balcony over the Prado. A chandelier of crystal, hanging by a chain from the remote ceiling, with a frosted sparkle like an illuminated wedding cake, unaffected by prismatic green and red flashes, filled the interior with a chilly brightness. The chairs of pale gilt set in a circle, the marble pattern of the floor, the dark heads of the Escobars, looked as though they were bathed in a vitreous fluid preserving them in a hard pallor forever.

But it was cool; the beginning constant night breeze fluttered the window curtains and swayed the pennants of smoke from the cigars. Domingo Escobar finished what was evidently a satirical period with a decisive clearing of his throat—a-ha! He was a small rotund man with a gigantic moustache laid without a brown hair misplaced over a mouth kindly and petulant. His wife, Carmita, obese with indulgent indolence, her placid expression faintly acid, waved a little hand, like a blanched almond, indicative of her endless surprise at the clamor of men. Andrés was silent, immobile, faultless in a severity of black and white.

Charles had begun to admire him inordinately

above everything, Andrés possessed a simple warmness of heart, a generosity of emotion, together with a fastidious mind. Fortunate combination. And his person, his gestures and flashing speech, his brooding, were invested by an intangible quality of romance; whatever he did was absorbing, dramatic and— and fateful. He was a trifle aloof, in spite of his impulsive humanity, a thought withdrawn as though by a shadow that might have been but his unfailing dignity.

Charles' gaze wandered from him to Narcisa, who, Domingo Escobar had said, resembled a flower bud. As she sat in pale yellow ruffles, with her slim hands clasped and her composed face framed in a wide dense stream of hair, she was decidedly fetching. Or, rather, she gave promise of charm; at present, she was too young to engage him in any considerable degree. Narcisa, he concluded, was fourteen. At very long intervals she looked up and he caught a lustrous, momentary interrogation of big black eyes. A very satisfactory sister for Andrés Escobar to have; and, wondering at the absence of Vincente, the eldest son, Charles asked Andrés about his brother.

A marked constraint was immediately visible in the family around him. Vincente, he was informed abruptly, was out of Havana, he had had to go to Matanzas. Later, on the balcony over the Prado, Andrés added an absorbing detail. "Vincente, we think, is in the Party of Liberation. But you must say nothing. I do not know, Vincente will not speak; but mama has noticed the gendarmes in front of the house, and when she drives."

"I should like to talk to him," Charles Abbott declared; "you must arrange it for me. Look here, there's nobody around, I might as well tell you that's why I came to Cuba, to fight the cursed Spanish. I'm—I'm serious, there's nothing I wouldn't do; and if I have to be killed, why, I am ready for that. It's all worked out in my head, except some petty little details. Cuba ought to be free; this oppression is horrible, like a spell on you—you're all afraid to more than whisper—that must be broken. It must! I have a good little bit of money and I can get more. You've got to help me."

Andrés clasped his hand. "That is wonderful!" His lowered exclamation vibrated with feeling. "How can you have such nobility! I am given to it, and Jaime and Remigio Florez and Tirso. But we are going to wait, we think that is better; Spain shall pay us when the time

THE BRIGHT SHAWL

comes. Those students, eight of them, who were shot, were well known to us. They put them against a wall by the prison and fired. You could hear it clearly. But, when we are ready, the Spanish Volunteers—" hatred closed his throat, drew him up rigidly. "Not yet," he insisted; "this shall be different, forever. Perhaps your country will help us then."

Charles was increasingly impatient; he couldn't, he felt, wait, delay his gesture for freedom. He conceived the idea that he might kill the Captain-General of Spain in Cuba, shoot him from the step of his carriage and cry that it was a memorial of the innocent boys he had murdered. Andrés dissuaded him; it would, he said, only make the conditions of living more difficult, harsh, put off the other, the final, consummation.

Below, on the promenade the rows of gas lamps shone wanly through the close leaves of the India laurels; there was a ceaseless sauntering throng of men; then, from the Plaza de Armas, there was the hollow rattat of drums, of tattoo. It was nine o'clock. The night was magnificent, and Charles Abbott was choked by his emotions; it seemed to him that his heart must burst with its expanding desire of heroic

[49]

good. He had left the earth for cloudy glories, his blood turned to a silver essence distilled in ethereal honor; he was no longer a body, but a vow, a purpose.

One thing, in a surpassing humility, he decided, and turned to Andrés. "Very well, if you think the other is best. Listen to me: I swear never to leave Cuba, never to have a different thought or a hope, never to consider myself at all, until you are free."

The intent face of Andrés Escobar, dim in the gloom of the balcony, was like a holy seal upon his dedication. A clatter of hoofs rose from below—the passage of a squad of the gendarmes on grey horses, their white coats a chalky glimmer in the night. Andrés and Charles watched them until they vanished toward the Parque Isabel; then Andrés swore, softly.

Again in his room at the Inglaterra Charles speculated about the complications of his determination to stay in Cuba until it was liberated from Spain. That, he began to realize, might require years. Questions far more difficult rose than any created by a mere immediate sacrifice; the attitude of his father, for example; he, conceivably, would try to force him home, shut off the supply of money. Meanwhile, since the Inglaterra was quite expensive, he would move to a less pretentious place. And, in the morning, Charles installed himself at the Hotel San Felipe, kept on Ancha del Norte Street, near the bay, by a German woman.

His room was on the top floor, on, really, a gallery leading to the open roof that was much frequented after dinner in a cooling air which bore the restrained masculine chords of guitars. On the right he could see the flares of Morro Castle, and, farther, the western coast lying black on the sea. He had his room there, and the first breakfast, but his formal breakfast and dinner he took at the Restaurant Français, the Aguila d'Oro, or the Café Dominica. Late, with Andrés and their circle, their tertulia, Charles would idle at the El Louvre over ice-cream or the sherbets called helados in Havana. On such occasions they talked with a studied audible care of the most frivolous things; while Charles cherished close at heart the sensation of their dangerous secret and patient wisdom, the assurance that some day their sacred resolution would like lightning shatter their pretence of docility.

*

*　　　　　*

Yet, in spite of the dark texture of their minds, they were, at times, casually happy, intent, together, on mundane affairs. They were, all five, inseparable: Jaime Quintara, the eldest, was even more of an exquisite than Andrés; he imported his lemon-colored gloves by the box from Paris, where they were made to his measure; and in them, it was the common jest, he went to bed. He was almost fat, with absurdly small feet and a perceptible moustache. In addition, he was in love with a public girl who lived on Gloria Street; altogether he was a man of the world. Remigio Florez was absolutely different: the son of a great coffee estate in Pinar del Rio, of limitless riches, he was still simple and unaffected, short, with a round cheerful face and innocent lips. Tirso Labrador was tall and heavy, he had the carriage of a cavalry officer, a dragoon; and, slow mentally, his chief characteristic was a remarkable steadfastness, a loyalty of friendship, admiration, for his more brilliant companions. Tirso Labrador was very strong, and it was his boast, when they were alone, that he intended to choke a Spaniard slowly to death with his naked hands.

Except, however, for the evening, Charles was rarely idle; upheld by his fervor he studied

[52]

THE BRIGHT SHAWL

Spanish with an instructor through most of the morning, and rode or fenced in the sala in the afternoon. His knowledge of Spanish, supplemented by his friends, grew rapidly; he had, his teacher declared, a very special aptitude for the language. Domingo Escobar got great delight from throwing sentences, queries, at him with inconceivable rapidity, and in pretending that every reply Charles attempted was senseless.

Narcisa, when he was present, contrived to sit with her gaze on her hands folded in her ruffled lap and to lift her widely opened eyes for breathless interrogations. She was, Charles was forced to admit, notably pretty; in fact, for a little girl, she was a beauty. Now if she had been thirty he might have had a hopeless passion for her, hopeless not because she failed to return it, but for the reason that he was a man without a future—some day, they both knew, he would desert love for stark death.

They went, Charles and Andrés, Tirso and Remigio and Jaime, to the Tacon Theatre for every play, where they occupied a box in the first row, the primer piso, and lounged, between the acts, on the velvet rail with their high silk hats and canes and boutonnières. At times there were capital troupes of players and dancers from An-

dalusia, and the evening was well spent. They
liked, too, the zarzuelas, the operettas of one act,
largely improvised with local allusions. But they
most warmly applauded the dancers.

One, La Clavel, from Seville, had been announced by posters all over the city; and, at the
moment she appeared on the Tacon stage, Tirso
had his heavy arm about Remigio's shoulders,
Jaime's gloved hands were draped over his cane,
and Charles was sitting in the rear of the box
with Andrés. The orchestra began a sharply
accented dance measure—it was a jota—and a
lithe figure in a mantón of blazing silks and a
raked black felt hat made a sultry bow.

La Clavel was indolent; she tapped a heel
and sounded her castanets experimentally; a
reminiscent smile hovered on the sombre beauty
of her face. Suddenly Charles' attention was
wholly captured by the dancer; he leaned forward, gazing over Remigio's shoulder, vaguely
conscious of the sound of guitars and suppressed
drums, the insistent ring of a triangle. She
stamped her foot now, and the castanets were
sharp, exasperated. Then slowly she began to
dance.

She wove a design of simple grace with her
hips still and her arms lifted and swaying; she

leaned back, her eyes, under the slanted brim of her hat, half closed; and her movements, the rhythm, grew more pronounced. Through the music Charles could hear the stamp of her heels, the augmented shrilling of the castanets. Her fire increased; there were great scarlet peonies on her shawl, and they fluttered as though they were troubled by a rising wind. La Clavel swept in a widening circle on her hips, and her arms were now extended and now thrust down rigidly behind her.

She dominated the cruel colors of her shawl with a savage intensity that made them but the expressions of her feelings—the scarlet and magenta and burning orange and blue were her visible moods, her capriciousness and contempt and variability and searing passion. Her hat was flung across the stage, and, with her bound hair shaking loose from its high shell comb, she swept into an appalling fury, a tormented human flame, of ecstasy. When Charles Abbott felt that he could support it no longer, suddenly she was, apparently, frozen in the immobility of a stone; the knotted fringe of her mantón hung without a quiver.

An uproar of applause rose from the theatre, a confusion of cries, of Olé! Olé!

Anda! Anda! Chiquella! A flight of
men's hats sailed like birds around her. Jaime
Quintara pounded his cane until it broke, and,
with the others, Charles shouted his unrestrained
Spanish approbation. They crowded into the
front of the box, intent on every movement, every
aspect, of the dancer. Afterwards, at the Tuileries, Andrés expressed their concerted feeling:

"The most magnificent woman alive!"

Jaime went across the café to speak to a man
who had a connection with the Tacon Theatre.
He returned with an assortment of information—
La Clavel was staying at the St. Louis; she would
be in Havana for a month; and she had been seen
with Captain Ceaza y Santacilla, of the regiment
of Isabel II. This latter fact cast them into a
gloom; and Remigio Florez so far broke the ban
of sustained caution as to swear, in the name of
the Lady of Caridad, at Santacilla and his kind.

Nothing, though, could reduce their enthusiasm for La Clavel; they worshipped her sever-
ally and together, discussing to the last shading
her every characteristic. She was young, but already the greatest dancer the world had—would
ever have, Charles added. And Andrés was instructed to secure the box for her every appearance in Havana; they must learn, they decided,

if she were to dance in Santiago de Cuba, in Mexico City, Rio de Janeiro, Lima, in Cathay. They, if it were mortally possible, would be present. Meanwhile none of them was to take advantage of the others in the contingency that she should miraculously come to love him. That incredible happiness the individual must sacrifice to his friendship, to his oath above all other oaths—Cuba. The country's name was not spoken, but it was entirely understood.

They were seated on the lower floor, by the stairs which led up to the salon for women; and, sharply, Charles grasped Andrés' arm. Passing them was a slender woman muffled in a black silk capote, with no hat to cover the intricate mass of her hair piled against a high comb. Behind her strode a Spanish officer of cavalry, his burnished scabbard hooked on his belt against its silver chain; short, with a thick sanguine neck above the band of his tunic, he had morose pale blue eyes and the red hair of compounded but distinct bloods.

"La Clavel," Charles whispered; "and it must be that filthy captain, Santacilla, with her."

*

*   *

THE BRIGHT SHAWL

Seated on the roof of the Hotel San Felipe, the night's trade wind faintly vibrant with steel strings, Charles Abbott thought at length about La Clavel. Two weeks had passed since she first danced at the Tacon Theatre; she had appeared on the stage three times afterward; and she was a great success, a prodigious favorite, in Havana. Charles and Andrés, Jaime and Remigio and Tirso Labrador, had, frankly, become infatuated with her; and it was this feeling which Charles, at present, was examining. If it endangered the other, his dedication to an ordeal of right, he had decided, he must resolutely put the dancer wholly outside his consideration.

This, he hoped, would not be necessary: his feeling for La Clavel lay in the realm of the impersonal. It was, in fact, parallel with the other supreme cause. La Clavel was a glittering thing of beauty, the perfection of all that—in a happier world, an Elysium—life and romance might be. He regarded her in a mood of decided melancholy as something greatly desirable and never to be grasped. When she danced his every sensibility was intensified; life, for the moment, was immeasurably lovely, flooded with lyrical splendor, vivid with gorgeous color and aching happiness. Charles' pleasure in every circumstance of being was acutely expanded—his affection for Andrés, the charm of Havana, the dignity of his impending fate.

Ordinarily he would not have been content with this; he would have striven to turn such abstractions into the concrete of an actual experience. But now an unusual wisdom held him intent on the vision; that, he recognized, was real; but what the reality, the woman herself, was, who could be sure? No, he wasn't in love with La Clavel in the accepted sense of that indefinite term; he was the slave of the illusion, the emotions, she spun; he adored her as the goddess of his youth and aspirations.

He tried to explain this, in halting and inadequate Spanish, to his tertulia; and because of his spirit rather than his words, his friends understood him. They were standing by the marble statue of Ferdinand VII in the Plaza de Armas, waiting for the ceremony of Retrata, to begin in a few moments. The square was made of four gardens, separated by formal walks, with a circular glorieta; and the gardens, the royal palms and banyans and flambeau trees, were palely lighted by gas lamps which showed, too, the circling procession of carriages about the Plaza. The square itself was filled with sauntering men, a shifting pattern of white linens, broad hats and glimmering cigars, diversified by the uniforms of Spain.

At eight o'clock a sergeant's guard and the band marched smartly into position before the Governor-General's palace, where they stood at rest until the drums of the barracks announced retreat. Then, at attention, the gun of El Morro sounded, and the band swept into the strains of Philemon et Baucis.

Jaime Quintara smiled sceptically at Charles' periods: Platonic sentiments might satisfy Abbott, he declared, but for himself. . . . At this, Remigio insisted on their moving out to inspect the carriages. They were, for the most part, quitrins, drawn with two horses, one outside the shafts ridden by a calesero in crimson velvet laced with gold and a glazed hat. The quitrins had two wheels, a leather hood strapped back, and held three passengers by means of a small additional seat, called, Andrés explained, la niña bonita, where the prettiest woman was invariably placed. None of the women wore hats, but they were nearly all veiled, and the carriages were burdened with seductive figures in wide dresses of perfumed white waving slow fans.

There was, however, little conversation be-

tween the men on foot and the women carefully
cultivating expressions of remote unconcern.
Rarely, if she were accompanied by a masculine
member of her family, a woman came to earth
for a short stroll in the gardens. Charles was
absolutely inattentive to them, but his companions, particularly Tirso and Jaime, noted and,
with dismaying freedom, commented on every
feminine detail that struck their fancy. It was
Tirso who excitedly called their attention to one
of the new volantas in which sat La Clavel.
Ceaza y Santacilla was not with her; the place at
her side was occupied by the man to whom Jaime
had spoken about the dancer in the Tuileries.
Quintara, capturing his attention, spoke in his
profoundest manner. There was a halt in the
movement of carriages, and La Clavel was directly before them.

She wore the high comb and a mantilla of
black lace falling in scalloped folds around the
vivid flower of her face—her beauty, at least to
Charles, was so extraordinary, her dark loveliness was so flaming, that the scarlet camellia in
her hair seemed wan. They were, all four, presented to the dancer; and four extreme bows, four
fervid and sonorous acknowledgments, rose to
the grace, the divinity, above. It seemed to

Charles that, perhaps because he was an American, La Clavel noticed him more than the others: certainly she smiled at him and the brilliancy of her gaze was veiled, made enigmatic, by the lowering of her sweeping eyelashes.

The checked restlessness of the horses was again released in a deliberate progress, but, as La Clavel was carried on, the man with her added that, after Retreta, they would stop at the El Louvre for an ice cream, a mantecado. Remigio Florez drew in a deep breath which he allowed to escape in the form of a sigh; Jaime smoothed the wrists of his bright yellow gloves; Tirso Labrador settled his guardsman's shoulders into his coat. "She won't get out of the volanta," Charles said thoughtfully; "and someone will have to bring out her refresco. We'd better get there early and stand at the door."

"No hurry," the suave Jaime put in; no one will leave here until after tattoo."

At nine o'clock the drums and bugles sounded from various parts of the city. There was one more tune played directly under the palace windows, after which the band and its guards left briskly to the measure of a quickstep. Charles led the way through the crowd to the Prado and the Parque Isabel. A number of carriages were there before them, the occupants mostly eating ices, and the café was being rapidly filled. Waiting keen-eyed at the entrance, they saw the volante with La Clavel before it drew up, and the calesero had scarcely dismounted from his horse when the dancer was offered her choice of the available sweets. She preferred, rather than an ice, an orchata, and sipped it slowly with an air of complete enjoyment. Her every movement, Charles Abbott saw, the turn of the hand holding the glass, her chin and throat against the black film of lace, her slender body's poise, was utterly and strongly graceful: it was, more than any other quality, the vigor of her beauty that impressed him. It seemed as though she must be superbly young, and dance magnificently, forever.

As Charles was considering this he was unceremoniously thrust aside for the passage of Captain Santacilla with another cavalry officer whose cinnamon colored face was stamped with sultry ill-humor. Santacilla addressed the dancer aggressively with the query of why she misspent her evening with the cursed Cuban negroes.

*

*   *

La Clavel made no reply, but tended her

empty glass to Andrés; then she glanced indifferently at the captains. "Their manners," she said, "are very pretty; and as for the negro—" she shrugged her delectable shoulders.

"My blood is as pure, as Castilian, as your own," Tirso Labrador began hotly; but Remigio stilled him with a hand on his arm. In an uncolored voice he begged the dancer to excuse them; and, sweeping off their hats, they were leaving when Santacilla's companion stepped forward in a flash of ungoverned anger like an exposed knife:

"I've noticed you before," he addressed Tirso, "hanging and gabbling around the cafés and theatres, and it's my opinion you are an insurrectionist. If the truth were known, I dare say, it would be found you are a friend to Cespedes. Anyhow, I'm tired of looking at you; if you are not more retiring, you will find yourself in the Cabañas."

"Good evening," Remigio repeated in an even tone. With his hand still on Tirso's arm he tried to force him into the café; but the other, dark with passion, broke away.

"You have dishonored my father and the name of a heroic patriot," he said to the officer of cavalry. "In this I am alone." With a suspicious quickness he leaned forward and his big hands shut about the Spaniard's throat.

Charles, with a suppressed exclamation, recalled Tirso's determination to choke one of the enemies of Cuba. The man in the gripping fingers stiffened and then, grotesquely, lost his aspect of a human form; suddenly he was no more than a thing of limp flesh and gay fabrics. Instantly an uproar, a surging passionate excitement grew, at the heart of which Tirso Labrador was curiously still. Heaving bodies, at once closing in and prudently scattering, hid from Charles his friend. There was an onrush of gendarmes, harsh exclamations and oaths; then, at the flash of steel, a short agonized cry—Tirso's voice at once hoarse and inhuman with death.

Charles Abbott, hurrying away at Andrés' urgent insistence, caught a final glimpse of a big young body sunk on the flagging of the Paseo; he saw a leaden face and a bubbling tide of blood. Beyond the Montserrat gate they halted, and he was shocked to hear Remigio Florez curse Tirso as brutally as any Spaniard. Andrés, white and trembling, agreed. "Here is what I warned you of," he turned to Charles; "it is fatal to lose your temper. You think that what Tirso did ends with him in purgatory . . . ha! Perhaps

[65]

he is best out of it among us all. It might be better for you to go back to America tomorrow and forget about Cuba."

"Yes," Remigio added, "probably we are all ruined; and certainly the police spies will be waiting for us at home."

"It would have been better if we had dissipated more," Jaime added: "we have been entirely too high-minded and unnatural. Young men meet together only to conspire or find love —the Spaniards know that—and we were fools."

"We haven't been suspected of anything," Andrés pointed out; "and it may be said that Tirso was killed defending his name. No, the trouble is to come; and it wasn't our fault. We must see less of each other, at least in public, and be quite overcome about Tirso; that is another account I charge to Spain: I knew him when I was a child . . . in the Vuelta Arriba—" Andrés Escobar began to cry wholly and unaffectedly; he leaned against an angle of the gate, his head in an arm, and prolonged sobs shook his body. Tears were silently streaming over Jaime's face, but Charles Abbott's eyes were dry. He was filled by an ecstasy of horror and detestation at the brutal murder of Tirso. Fear closed his throat

[66]

and pinched his heart with icy fingers; but he ignored, rose above, himself, in a tremendous accession of his determination to drive injustice— if not yet from the world—from Cuba.

How little, he thought, anyone knew him who advised a return to America. Before the cold violent fact of death a great part of his early melodramatic spirit evaporated; the last possible trace of any self-glorification left him, the lingering mock-heroics of boyhood were gone. His emotion, now, was almost exultant; like a blaze of insuperable white light it drowned all the individual colors of his personality; it appeared to him almost that he had left the earth, that he was above other men.

More than anything, he continued, he would require wisdom, the wisdom of patience, maturity; Tirso had been completely wasted. He was seated, again, on the roof of his hotel, and again it was night: the guitars were like a distant sounding of events evolved in harmonies, and there was the gleam of moonlight on the sea, a trace of the moon and the scent of mignonette trees.

He was, he felt, very old, grave, in deportment; this detachment from living must be the mark of age. Charles had always been a little removed from activity by sickness; and now his almost solitary, dreaming habit of existence had deepened in him. He thought, from time to time, of other periods than his own, of ages when such service as his had been, for gentlemen, the commonplace of living: he saw, in imagination, before the altar of a little chapel, under the glimmer of tall candles, a boyish figure kneeling in armor throughout the night. At morning, with a faint clashing of steel, the young knight under a vow rode into black forests of enchanted beasts and men and impure magic, from which he delivered the innocent and the pure in heart.

Charles Abbott recalled the burning of the Protestant Cranmer, and, as well, the execution of John Felton for posting the Papal bull against the Queen on the door of London House. They too, like the knights of Arthurian legend, had conquered the flesh for an ideal. He was carried in spirit into a whole world of transcendent courage, into a company who scorned ease and safety in the preservation of an integrity, a devotion, above self. This gave him a release, the sense that his body was immaterial, that filled him with a calm serious fervor.

He was conscious, through this, of the ceaseless playing of the guitars, strains of jotas and malagueñas, laden with the seductiveness, the fascination, of sensuous warm life. It was, in its persistence, mocking; and finally it grew into a bitter undertone to the elevation of his thought: he wanted, like Savonarola, to bring to an end the depravity of the city; he wanted to cleanse Havana of everything but the blanched heavenly ardor of his own dedication. The jotas continued and the scent of mignonette increased. The moon, slipping over the sea, shone with a vague brightness on the leaves of the laurels below, on the whiteness of marble walks, and in the liquid gleam of fountains. A woman laughed with a note of uncertainty and passion. . . . It was all infinitely removed from him, not of the slightest moment. What rose, dwelt, in Charles was a breath of eternity, of infinitude; he was lost in a vision of good beyond seasons, changeless, and for all men whomsoever. It must come, he told himself so tensely that he was certain he had cried his conviction aloud. The music sustained its burden of earthly desire to which the harsh whispering rustle of the palm fronds added a sound like a scoffing laughter.

*

*   *

69

At the Plaza de Toros, the following Sunday afternoon, Charles saw La Clavel; she was seated on an upper tier near the stand of the musicians, over the entrance for the bulls; and, in an audience composed almost entirely of men, she was brilliantly conspicuous in a flaming green mantón embroidered in white petals; her mantilla was white, and Charles could distinguish the crimson blot of the flower by her cheek. The brass horns and drums of the band were making a rasping uproar, and the crowded wooden amphitheatre was tense with excitement. Andrés Escobar, beside Charles, was being gradually won from a settled melancholy; and, in an interested voice, he spoke to Charles about the espada, José Ponce, who had not yet killed a bull in Cuba, but who was a great hero of the ring in Spain and South America.

"There is La Clavel," Charles said by way of reply; "she is with Captain Santacilla, and I think, but I can't be sure, the officer Tirso tried to choke to death. What is his name—de Vaca, Gaspar Arco de Vaca."

"Even that," Andrés answered, "wasn't accomplished. La Clavel's engagement in Havana is over; I suppose it will be Buenos Aires next. Do you remember how we swore to follow her all

[70]

over the world, and how Tirso wanted to drag
her volanta in place of the horses? At heart, it's
no doubt, she is Spanish, and yet. . . . There's
the procession."

The key bearer, splendid in velvet and gold
and silver, with a short cloak, rode into the ring
followed by the picadores on broken-down horses:
their legs were swathed in leather and their
jackets, of ruby and orange and emerald, were
set with expensive lace. They carried pikes with
iron points; while the banderilleros, on foot, with
hair long and knotted like a woman's, hung their
bright cloaks over an arm and bore the darts gay
with paper rosettes.

The espada, José Ponce, was greeted with a
savage roar of approbation; he was dressed in
green velvet, his zouave jacket heavy with gold
bullion; and his lithe slender dark grace recalled
to Charles Abbott La Clavel. Charles paid little
attention to the bull fighting, for he was far in
the sky of his altruism; his presence at the Plaza
de Toros was merely mechanical, the routine of
his life in Havana. Across from him the banked
humanity in the cheaper seats à sol, exposed to the
full blaze of mid-afternoon, made a pattern without individual significance; he heard the quick
bells of the mules that dragged out the dead

bulls; a thick revolting odor rose from the hot sand soaked with the blood and entrails of horses.

At times, half turning, he saw the brilliant shawl of the dancer, and more than once he distinguished her voice in the applause following a specially skilful or daring pass. He thought of her with a passionate admiration unaffected by the realization that she had brought them the worst of luck: perhaps any touch of Spain was corrupting, fatal. And the sudden desire seized him to talk to La Clavel and make sure that her superb art was unshadowed by the disturbing possibilities voiced by Andrés.

There were cries of fuego! fuego! and Charles Abbott was conscious of a bull who had proved indifferent to sport. A banderillero, fluttering his cloak, stepped forward and planted in the beast's shoulder a dart that exploded loudly with a spurt of flame and smoke; there was a smothered bellow, and renewed activities went forward below. "What a rotten show!" Charles said to Andrés, and the latter accused him of being a tender sentimentalist. José Ponce, Andrés pronounced with satisfaction, was a great sword. The espada was about to kill: he moved as gracefully as though he were in the figure of a dance; his thrust, as direct as a flash of lightning, went

[72]

up to the hilt, and the vomiting bull fell in crashing death at his feet.

"Suppose, for a change, we go to the Aguila de Oro," Andrés suggested; "the air is better there." By that he meant that the café was relatively free from Spaniards. The throng moved shoulder to shoulder slowly to the doors; but Charles managed to work his way constantly nearer the conspicuous figure of La Clavel. He despaired, however, of getting close to her, when an unforeseen eddy of humanity separated the dancer from her companions and threw her into Charles' path. She recognized him immediately: but, checking his formal salutation, she said, in a rapid lowered voice, that she would very much like to see him . . . at the St. Louis late on the afternoon of tomorrow. They were separated immediately, leaving in Charles a sense of excited anticipation. He joined Andrés soon after and told him what had occurred.

"I suppose it is safe for you," Andrés decided; "you are an American, no one has yet connected you with the cause of Cuba. But this woman—What do we know of her?—you'll have to be prudent!"

Andrés Escobar had grown severe in the last week, he had hardened remarkably; his concentration, Charles felt, his bitterness, even excluded his friends. Charles Abbott's affection for him increased daily; his love, really, for Andrés was a part of all that was highest in him. Unlike the love of any woman, Andrés made no demand on him, what only mattered was what each intrinsically was: there were no pretence, no weary protestations, nothing beside the truth of their mutual regard, their friendship. What Charles possessed belonged equally, without demand, to Andrés; they had, aside from their great preoccupation, the same thoughts and prejudices, the same taste in refrescos and beauty and clothes. They discovered fresh identical tastes with a rush of happiness.

It was, like the absorbing rest, immaterial, the negation of ordinary aims and ideas of comfort and self-seeking. Charles would have died for Andrés, Andrés for Charles, without a moment's hesitation; indeed, the base of their feeling lay in the full recognition of that fact. This they admitted simply, with no accent of exaggeration or boasting: on the present plane of their being it was the most natural thing in the world.

At the Aguila de Oro, spinning the paddle of a molinillo, an individual chocolate mill, Andrés informed Charles that Vincente was home. "He

has told me everything," Andrés Escobar continued with pride. "We are now more than Escobars—brother Cubans. He has been both shot
and sabred and he has a malaria. But nearly all
his friends are dead. Soon, he says, we, Jaime
and Remigio—and, I added, you—will have to
go out. He is to let us know when and how."

"Do the police know he is in Havana?"

"We think not; they haven't been about the
house since the investigation of the de Vaca
affair, and our servants are not spies. You must
come and see Vincente this evening, for he may
leave at any hour. It seems that he is celebrated
for his bravery and the Spaniards have marked
him for special attention. Papa and mama are
dreadfully disturbed, and not only because of
him; for if he is discovered, all of us, yes, little
Narcisa, will be made to pay—to a horrible degree, I can tell you."

*

*　　　　　*

There was, apparently, nothing unusual in the
situation at the Escobars' when Charles called in
the evening. The family, exactly as he had
known it, was assembled in the drawing-room,
conversing under the icy flood of the crystal chan-

delier. He found a chair by Narcisa, and listened studiously to the colloquial Spanish, running swiftly around the circle, alternating with small thoughtful silences. Soon, however, Charles Abbott could see that the atmosphere was not normal—the vivacity palpably was forced through the shadow of a secret apprehension. Domingo Escobar made sudden seemingly irrelevant gestures, Carmita sighed out of her rotundity. Only Narcisa was beyond the general subdued gloom: in her clear white dress, her clocked white silk stockings, and the spread densely black curtain of her hair, she was intent on a wondering thought of her own. Her gaze, as usual, was lowered to her loosely clasped hands; but, growing conscious of Charles' regard, she looked up quickly, and, holding his eyes, smiled at him with an incomprehensible sweetness.

He regarded her with a gravity no more than half actual—his mind was set upon Vincente—and her even pallor was invaded by a slow soft color. Charles nodded, entirely friendly, and she turned away, so abruptly that her hair swung out and momentarily hid her profile. He forgot her immediately, for he had overheard, half understood, an allusion to the Escobars' elder son. With a growing impatience he interrogated

Andrés, and the latter nodded a reassurance. Then Andrés Escobar rose, punctiliously facing his father—he would, with permission, take Charles to the upper balconies, the wide view from which he had never seen. Domingo was plainly uneasy, displeased; but, after a long frowning pause, gave his reluctant consent. Charles Abbott was acutely aware of his heels striking against the marble steps which, broad, imposing and dark, led above. Vincente, it developed, without actually being in hiding, was limited to the scope of the upper hall, where, partly screened in growing palms, its end formed a small salon.

There was a glimmer of light though sword-like leaves, and a lamp on an alabaster table set in ormolu cast up its illumination on a face from which every emotion had been banished by a supreme weariness. Undoubtedly at one time Vincente Escobar had been as handsome as Andrés; more arbitrary, perhaps, with a touch of impatience resembling petulance; the carriage, the air, of a youth spoiled by unrestrained inclination and society. The ghost of this still lingered over him, in the movement of his slender hands, the sharp upflinging of his chin; but it was no more than a memento of a gay and utterly

lost past. The weariness, Charles began to realize, was the result of more than a spent physical
and mental being—Vincente was ill. He had
acquired a fever, it was brought out, in the
jungles of Camagüey.

At first he was wholly indifferent to Charles;
at the end of Andrés' enthusiastic introduction,
after a flawless but perfunctory courtesy, Vincente
said:

"The United States is very important to us; we
have had to depend almost entirely on the New
York Junta for our life. We have hope, too, in
General Grant. Finally your country, that was
so successful in its liberation, will understand us
completely, and sweep Spain over the sea. But,
until that comes, we need only money and courage in our, in Cuban, hearts. You are, I understand from Andrés, rich; and you are generous,
you will give?"

That direct question, together with its hint at
the personal unimportance of his attachment to
a cause of pure justice, filled Charles with both
resentment and discomfort. He replied stiffly,
in halting but adequate Spanish, that there had
been a misunderstanding: "I am not rich; the
money I have you would think nothing—it might
buy a stand or two of rifles, but no more. What

[78]

I had wanted to spend was myself, my belief in Cuba. It seemed to me that might be worth something—" he stopped, in the difficulty of giving expression to his deep convictions; and Andrés warmly grasped his hand. He held Charles' palm and addressed his brother in a passionate flood of protest and assertion: Charles Abbott, his dear friend, was as good a patriot as any Escobar, and they should all embrace him in gratitude and welcome; he was, if not the gold of the United States, its unselfish and devoted heart; his presence here, his belief in them, was an indication of what must follow.

"If he were killed," Andrés explained. "That alone would bring us an army; the indignation of his land would fall like a mountain on our enemies."

This, giving Charles a fresh view of his usefulness, slightly cooled his ardor; he was willing to accept it, in his exalted state he would make any sacrifice for the ideal that had possessed him; but there was an acceptance of brutal unsentimental fact in the Latin fibre of the Escobars foreign to his own more romantic conceptions. Vincente wasn't much carried away by the possibility Andrés revealed.

"He'd be got out of the way privately," he explained in his drained voice; "polite letters and no more, regrets, would be exchanged. The politicians of Washington are not different from those of Cuba. If he is wise he will see Havana as an idler. Even you, Andrés, do not know yet what is waiting for you. It is one thing to conspire in a balcony on the Prado and another to lie in the marshes of Camagüey. You cannot realize how desperate Spain is with the debt left from her wars with Morocco and Chile and Peru. Cuba, for a number of years, has been her richest possession. While the Spaniards were paying taxes of three dollars and twenty some cents, we, in Cuba, were paying six dollars and sixtynine. After our declaration of independence at Manzanillo—" an eloquent pause left his hearers to the contemplation of what had followed.

"You know how it has gone with us," Vincente continued, almost exclusively to the younger Escobar. "Carlos Cespedes left his practice of the law at Bayamo for a desperate effort with less than a hundred and thirty men. But they were successful, and in a few weeks we had fifteen thousand, with the constitution of a republican government drawn. We ended slavery," here, for a breath, he addressed Charles Abbott. "But in that," he specified, "we were different from you. In the United States slavery was considered as only a moral wrong. Your Civil War was, after all, an affair of philanthropy; while we freed the slaves for economic reasons.

"Well, our struggle went on," he returned to Andrés, "and we were victorious, with, at the most, fifty thousand men against how many? One, two, hundred thousand. And we began to be recognized abroad, by Bolivia and Columbia and the Mexican Congress. The best Cubans, those like ourselves, were in sympathy with the insurrection. Everything was bright, the climate, too, was fighting for us; and then, Andrés, we lost man after man, the bravest, the youngest, first: they were murdered, as I may be tonight, killed among the lianas, overtaken in the villages, smothered in small detachments by great forces, until now. And it is for that I have said so much, when it is unnecessary to pronounce a word. What do you think is our present situation? What do you think I left of our splendid effort in the interior? General Agramonte and thirty-five men. That and no more!

"Their condition you may see in me—wasted, hardly stronger than pigeons, and less than half armed. What, do you think, one boy from Pennsylvania is worth to that? Can he live without food more than half the time, without solid land under his feet, without protection against the mosquitoes and heat and tropical rains? And in Havana: but remember your friend, Tirso Labrador! You, Andrés, have no alternative; but your Charles Abbott—he would be a danger rather than an assistance." Charles, with a prodigious effort at a calm self-control, answered him.

"You are very thoughtful, and it is right to be cautious, but what you say is useless. Andrés understands! I'd never be satisfied to be anything except a Cuban patriot. It isn't necessary for you to understand that in a minute, an evening. I might be no good in Camagüey, but I am not as young as Tirso; I am more bitter and patient. By heaven, I will do something, I will be a part of your bravery! Not only the soldiers in the field, not only Agramonte, but sacrifice—"

*

*   *

Charles' throat was closed, his words stopped, by the intensity of his feeling; his longing to be identified, lost, in the spirit of General Agramonte and the faithful thirty-five burned into a

[82]

desperation of unhappiness. Vincente Escobar, it was evident, thought that he wasn't capable of sustaining such a trust. Still there was nothing to be gained by protests, hot asseverations; with difficulty he suppressed his resentment, and sat, to all appearances, calm, engaged with a cigar and attending Vincente's irregular vehement speech. Andrés was silent, dark and serious; but the gaze he turned upon Charles was warm with affection and admiration. Nothing, Vincente insisted, could be done now; they must wait and draw into their cause every possible ultimate assistance and understanding. If the truth were known, he repeated again and again, the world would be at their feet.

Finally, his enthusiasm, his power, ebbed; his yellow pinched face sank forward: he was so spent, so delivered to a loose indifference of body, that he might well have been dead. Charles rose with a formal Spanish period voicing the appreciation of the honor that had been his.

"We are all worried about Vincente," Andrés proceeded, as they were descending the vault-like stairs; "there is a shadow on him like bad luck. But it may be no more than the fever. Our mother thinks he needs only her love and enough wine jelly." They were again in the

[83]

drawing-room with the Escobars; and Charles momentarily resumed the seat he had left beside Narcisa.

Domingo and his wife were submerged in gloomy reflection, and Andrés sat with his gaze fixed on the marble, patterned in white and black, of the floor. Suddenly Narcisa raised her head with an air of rebellion. "It's always like the church," she declared incredibly. "Everything has got so old that I can't bear it—Vincente as good as dead and Andrés resembling a Jesuit father! Must all my life go on in this funeral march?" The elder Escobars regarded her in a voiceless amazement; but Andrés said severely:

"You are too young to understand the tragedy of Cuba or Vincente's heroic spirit. I am ashamed of you—before Charles Abbott."

Narcisa rose and walked swiftly out upon the balcony. They had been, it seemed to Charles, rather ridiculous with her; it was hard on Narcisa to have been thrust, at her age, into such a serious affair. The Escobars, and particularly Vincente, took their responsibility a little too ponderously. Following a vague impulse, made up both of his own slightly damaged pride and a sympathy for Narcisa, he went out to the balcony where she stood with her hands lightly resting on the railing. Veiled in the night, her youth seemed more mysterious than immature; he was conscious of an unsteady flutter at her unformed breast; her face had an aspect of tears.

"You mustn't mind them," he told her; "they are tremendously bothered because they see a great deal farther than you can. The danger to Vincente, too, in Havana, spies—"

She interrupted him, looking away so that he could see only a trace of her cheek against the fragment fall of her hair. "It isn't that, but what Andrés said about you."

This admission startled him, and he studied Narcisa—her hands now tightly clasping the iron railing—with a disturbed wonder. Was it possible that she cared for him? At home, ignored by a maturity such as his, she would have been absorbed in the trivial activities of girls of her own age. But Havana, the tropics, was different. It was significant, as well, that he was permitted to be with her, practically alone, beyond the sight and hearing of her mother; the Escobars, he thought, had hopes of such a consummation. It was useless, he was solely wedded to Cuba; he had already pictured the only dramatic accident of the heart that could touch him. Not little Narcisa! She was turned away from him completely: a lovely back, straight and narrow, virginal—Domingo Escobar had said this —as a white rose bud, yet with an impalpable and seductive scent. In other circumstances, a happier and more casual world, she would have been an adorable fate. An increasing awkwardness seized him, a conviction of impotence. "Narcisa," he whispered at her ear; but, before he could finish his sentence, her face was close to his, her eyes were shut and the tenderness of her lips unprotected.

Charles put an arm about her slim shoulders and pressed his cheek against hers. "Listen," he went on, in his lowered voice, patching the deficiencies of his Spanish with English words clear in their feeling if not in sound, "nothing could have shown me myself as well as you, for now I know that I can never give up a thought to anything outside what I have promised my life to. A great many men are quite happy with a loving wife and children and a home—a place to go back to always; and, in a way, since I have known you, I envy them. Their lives are full of happiness and usefulness and specially peace; but, dearest Narcisa, I can't be like that, it isn't for me. You see, I have chosen to love a country; instead of being devoted only to you, there are thousands of women, rich and poor and black and white, I must give myself for. I haven't any existence, any rights, of my own; I haven't any money or time or security to offer. I didn't choose it, no, it chose me—it's exactly as though I had been stopped on the street and conscripted. A bugle was blown in my ear. Love, you must realize, is selfish; it would be selfish to take you on a steamer, for myself, and go north. If I did that, if I forgot what I have sworn, I'd die. I should seem to the world to be alive, and I'd walk about and talk and go into the city on some business or other; but, in reality, I should be as dead as dust.

"There are men like that everywhere, Narcisa, perhaps the most of life is made up of them. They look all right and are generally respected; yet, at some time or other, they killed themselves, they avoided what they should have met, tried to save something not worth a thought. I don't doubt a lot never find it out, they think they are as good as ever—they don't remember how they once felt. But others discover it, or the people who love them discover it for them. And that would happen to me, to us."

In reply to all this she whispered that she loved him. Her arm slipped up across his shoulder and the tips of her fingers touched his left cheek. A momentary dizziness enveloped him at her immeasurable sweetness: it might be that she was a part of what he was to find, to do, in Cuba; and then his emotion perished in the bareness of his heart to physical passion. Its place was taken by a deep pride in his aloofness from the flesh; that alone, he felt, dignified him, set him above the mischances of self-betrayal.

Charles Abbott kissed her softly and then took her hands. "You wouldn't want me, Narcisa," he continued; "if I failed in this, I should fail you absolutely. If I were unfaithful now I could never be faithful to you."

She drew her hands sharply away. "It's you who are young and not I," she declared; "you talk like a boy, like Andrés. All you want is a kind of glory, like the gold lace the officers of Isabella wear. Nothing could be more selfish."

"You don't understand," he replied patiently.

Narcisa, he felt, could never grasp what was such a profound part of his masculine necessity. Abstractions, the liberty, for example, of an alien people, would have little weight against her instinct for the realities in her own heart. Her emotion was tangible, compared with his it was

deeply reasonable; it moved in the direction of
their immediate good, of the happiness, the full-
ness, of their beings; while all his desire, his
hope, was cloudy, of the sky. In the high silver
radiance of his idealism, the warmer green of
earth, the promise of Narcisa's delicate charm,
the young desire in his blood, were, he felt, far
away, dim . . . below.

*
*   *

The conviction fastened upon him that this
chance realization would determine, where women
were concerned, the whole of his life. But that
space, he reminded himself, short at best, was,
in him, to terminate almost at once. All his
philosophy of resistance, of strength, was built
upon the final dignity of a supreme giving. His
thoughts went back to Narcisa as he sat in La
Clavel's room in the St. Louis, watching a hair-
dresser skilfully build up the complicated edi-
fice of the dancer's hair. Soon, he grasped, it
would be ready for the camellia placed back of
the lobe of an ear. A towel was pinned about
her naked shoulders, she had on a black fringed
petticoat and dangling slippers of red morocco
leather. La Clavel was faced away from
Charles, but, in the mirror before which she sat,

he could see her features and vivid changing expressions.

The truth was that, close, he had found her disconcerting, almost appalling. Climbing the long stairs at the message that she would see him in her room, he had surrendered himself to the romantic devotion which had overwhelmed the small select circle of his intimates. This had nothing to do with the admirable sentiment of a practical all-inclusive love; it was æsthetic rather than social. They all worshipped La Clavel as a symbol of beauty, as fortunately unattainable in a small immediate measure; and, bowing inside the door of her chamber, he had been positively abashed at the strange actuality of her charm.

La Clavel was at once more essentially feminine than any other woman he had encountered and different from all the rest. A part of the impression she created was the result of her pallor, the even unnatural whiteness under the night of her hair. Her face was white, but her lips —a carmine stick lay close at her hands—were brutally red. She hurt him, struck savagely at the idealism of his image; indeed, in the room permeated with a dry powdered scent, at the woman redolent of vital flesh, he had been a little sickened. However, that had gone; and he

watched the supple hands in the crisp coarse mass
of her hair with a sense of adventure lingering
faintly from his earlier youth: he was, in very
correct clothes, holding his hat and stick and
gloves, idling through the toilet of a celebrated
dancer and beauty.

Or, rather, he saw himself objectively, as he
had been say a year ago, at which time his present situation would have surpassed his most
splendid worldly hopes. It was strange, he
thought, how life granted one by one every desire . . . when it was no longer valued: the
fragrance, the tender passion, of Narcisa, the
preference in La Clavel singling him out from a
city for her interest!

She smiled at him over her shoulder, and, in
return, he nodded seriously, busy with a cigarette; maintaining, in a difficult pass, his complete
air of indifference, of experience. The hair-
dresser must have pulled roughly at a strand for,
with a sudden harsh vulgarity, she described
him as a blot on the virginity of his mother; in
an instant every atom of her was charged with
anger. It was, Charles told himself, exactly as
though a shock of dried grass had caught fire;
ignited gun powder rather than blood seemed to
fill her veins.

Her ill-temper, tempestuous in its course, was
over as quickly as it had flared into being. She
paid the hair-dresser from a confusion of silver
and gold on her dressing-table and dismissed
him with a good nature flavored by a native prov-
erb. Then, bending above a drawer, she
brought out the vivid shawl in which she had
danced. La Clavel folded its dragging brilliancy squarely along its length, laid it across
her breast, brought the fringed ends under and
up over her arms, crossed them in a swift twist,
and she was wholly, magnificently, clothed.
She sat on the edge of a bed covered with gay
oddments of attire—fans and slippers with vermilion heels, lace mantillas, a domino in silver tissue lined in carnation and a knife with a
narrow blade and holder of silk.

Charles offered her his cigarette case, but she
declined in favor of the long pale cigars Andrés
and he himself affected. With its smoke drifting bluely across her pallid face, her eyes now
interrogating him, and now withdrawn in
thought, she asked him about Tirso Labrador.
Charles Abbott quickly gathered that his presence
was for that sole purpose.

"I heard all that was said," she warned him;
"and I don't want that repeated. Why did he

try to garotte de Vaca with his hands? There was more in it than appeared. But all Ceaza will say is that he was a cursed traitor to the Crown. Signor American, I like Cuba, they have been very good to me here; I like you and your polite friends. But whenever I try to come closer to you, to leave the stage, as it were, for the audience, we are kept apart. The Spanish officers who take up so much of my time warn me that I must have nothing to do with disaffected Cubans; the Cubans, when I reach out my arms to them, are only polite.

"Certainly I know that there has been a rebellion; but it is stamped out, ended, now; there are no signs of it in Havana, when I dance the jota; so why isn't everyone sensible and social; why, if they are victorious, are not Gaspar Arco de Vaca and Ceaza y Santacilla easier? If, as it must be, Cuba is subjected, why doesn't it ignore the unpleasant and take what the days and nights always offer? There can be no longer, so late in the history of the world, a need for the old Inquisition, the stabbers Philip commanded."

Charles Abbott had an impulse to reply that, far from being conquered, the spirit of liberty in Cuba was higher than ever before; he wanted to tell her, to cry out, that it was deathless; and that no horrors of the black past were more appalling than those practiced now by the Spanish soldiery. Instead of this he watched a curl of smoke mount through the height of the room to a small square window far up on the wall where it was struck gold by a shaft of sunlight.

"He was particularly a friend of yours?" she insisted, returning to Tirso. "You were always together, watching me dance from your box in the Tacon Theatre, and eating ices at the El Louvre or at the Tuileries."

He spoke slowly, indifferently, keeping his gaze elevated toward the ceiling. "Tirso Labrador was a braggard, he was always boasting about what he could do with his foolish muscles. What happened to him was unavoidable. We weren't sorry—a thorough bully. As for the others, that dandy, Quintara, and Remigio Florez, who looks like a coffee berry from their plantation at Vuelta Arriba, and Escobar, I am very much in their debt—I bring the gold and they provide the pleasures of Havana. They are my runners. I haven't the slightest interest in their politics; if they support the Revolution or Madrid, they keep all that out of my knowledge."

A prolonged silence followed, a period devoted to the two cigars. "That Escobar," La Clavel said, "is a very beautiful boy. What you tell me is surprising; he, at any rate, seems quite different. And I have seen you time after time sitting together, the two or three or four of you, with affectionate glances and arms. I am sensitive to such things, and I think you are lying."

An air of amused surprise appeared on his countenance, "If you are so taken with Andrés Escobar," he observed, "why did you make this appointment with me? May I have the pleasure of taking him a note from you? he is very fond of intrigues."

Leaning forward she laid a firm square palm on his knee. "You have told me all that I wanted—this Tirso, who was killed, he was your dear friend and his death an agony; the smaller, the coffee berry, you are devoted to his goodness and simplicity; beneath Quintara's waistcoats you find a heart of gold. But Escobar—is it Andrés?—you love better than your life. They care nothing for your American dollars; it is evident they all have much more than you. What is it, then, you are united by? I shall tell you—Cuba. You are patriots, insurrectionists;

[95]

Santacilla was right. And neither is your rebellion crushed, not with Agramonte alive." She leaned back with glimmering eyes and the cruel paint of her mouth ·smiling at him.

*

* *

She was, then, Charles Abbott reflected, an agent of Spain's; calmly he rehearsed all they had said to each other, he examined every sentence, every inflection of voice. He could not have been more circumspect; the position he had taken, of a pleasure-loving young American, was so natural that it was inevitable. No, La Clavel knew nothing, she was simply adopting another method in her task of getting information for Santacilla. At this, remembering the adoration of his circle for her, he was brushed by a swift sorrow. For them she had been the symbol, the embodiment, of beauty; the fire and grace of her dancing had intensified, made richer, their sense of life. She had been the utmost flashing peak of their desire; and now it was clear to him that she was rotten at the core, La Clavel was merely a spy; what had engaged them was nothing more than a brilliant flowery surface, a bright shawl.

"You are wasting your efforts," he assured

her, with an appearance of complete comfort. "Even if you were right, I mean about the others, what, do you think, would make them confide in me, almost a stranger? You understand this so much better than I that, instead of questioning me, you ought to explain the whole Cuban situation. Women like yourself, with genius, know everything."

She utterly disconcerted Charles by enveloping him in a rapid gesture, her odorous lips were pressed against his cheek. "You are as sweet as a lime flower," La Clavel declared. "After the others—" her expression of disgust was singularly valid. "That is what I love about you," she cried suddenly, "your youth and freshness and courage. Tirso Labrador dying so gallantly . . . all your beardless intent faces. The revolt in Cuba, I've felt it ever since I landed at Havana, it's in the air like wine. I am sick of officers: look, ever since I was a child the army has forced itself upon me. I had to have their patronage when I was dancing and their company when I went to the cafés; and when it wasn't the cavalry it was the gentlemen. They were always superior, condescending; and always, inside me, I hated them. They thought, because I was peasant born, that their attentions filled me with

joy, that I should be grateful for their aristocratic presences. But, because I was what I was,
I held them, with their ladies' hands and sugared
voices, in contempt. There isn't one of them
with the entrails to demand my love.

"I tell you I was smothering in the air about
me. My dancing isn't like the posturing of the
court, it's the dancing of the people, my people,
passionate like a knife. I am from the Morena,
and there we are not the human sheep who
live in the valleys, along the empty rivers. How
shall I explain? But how can you explain yourself? You are not a Cuban; this rebellion, in
which you may so easily be killed almost before
you begin to live, it isn't yours. What drew you
into it? You must make it plain, for I, too, am
caught."

"Men are different from women," he replied,
putting into words his newly acquired wisdom;
"whatever happened to me would be useless for
you, you couldn't be helped by it." Yet he was
forced to admit to himself that all she had said
was reasonable; at bottom it didn't contradict his
generalization, for it was based on a reality, on
La Clavel's long resentment, on indignities to her
pride, on, as she had said, the innate freedom of
the mountain spirit. If she were honest, any

possible attachment to Cuba might result from her hatred of Spain, of Sevilla and Madrid. Hers, then, would be the motive of revenge.

"You are right about the difference in our experiences," she agreed; "I was dancing for a living at six; at ten I had another accomplishment. I have lived in rooms inlaid with gold, and in cellars with men where murder would have been a gracious virtue. Yes, lime flower, there is little you know that could be any assistance to me. But the other, your purity, your effort of nobility, that I must learn from you."

He explained his meaning more fully to her, and she listened intently. "You think," she interrupted, "that a woman must be attached to something real, like your arm or a pot of gold. You know them, and that at your age, at any age, is a marvel enough in itself. The wisest men in Europe have tried to understand the first movement of my dancing—how, in it, a race, the whole history of a nation, is expressed in the stamp of a heel, the turn of a hip. They wonder what, in me, had happened to the maternal instinct, why I chose to reflect life, as though I were a mirror, rather than experience it. And now, it seems, you see everything, all is clear to

[99]

you. You have put a label, such as are in museums, on women; good!"

She smiled at him, mocking but not unkind.

"However," he told her crossly, "that is of very little importance. How did we begin? I have forgotten already."

"In this way," she said coolly; "I asked if it would be of any interest to—let us say, your friends, to learn that the United States, in spite of the Administration, will not recognize a Republican Cuba. Fish is unchangeably opposed to the insurgents. You may expect no help there."

"That might be important to the insurgents," he admitted; "but where are they to be found— in the cabildos of Los Egidos?"

"At least repeat what you have heard to Escobar: is it Andrés or Vincente?"

The name of Andrés' brother was spoken so unexpectedly, the faintest knowledge of Vincente on the part of the dancer of such grave importance, that Charles Abbott momentarily lost his composure. "Vincente!" he exclaimed awkwardly. "Was that the other brother? But he is dead."

"Not yet," she replied. "It is planned for tonight, after dinner, when he is smoking in the little upper salon."

[100]

Agitated, at a loss for further protest, he rose. He must go at once to the Escobars, warn them. "You will admit now that I have been of use," La Clavel was standing beside him. "And it is possible, if Vincente Escobar isn't found, and Ceaza discovers that you were here, that—" she paused significantly. "I am the victim of a madness," she declared, "of a Cuban fever." But there was no time now to analyse the processes of her mind and sex.

"I'll be going," he said abruptly.

"Naturally," she returned; "but what about your coming back? That will be more difficult, and yet it is necessary. Ah, yes, you must pretend to be in love with me; it will be hard, but what else is there? A dancer has always a number of youths at her loose heels.

"You will be laughed at, of course; the officers, Santacilla and Gaspar, will be unbearable. You will have to play the infatuated fool, and send me bouquets of gardenias and three-cornered notes, and give me money. That won't be so hard, because we can use the same sum over and over; but I shall have to read the notes to my protectors in the army."

"I'll be going," he repeated, gathering his stick and gloves from the floor. She asked, with

[101]

a breath of wistfulness, if he could manage a touch of affection for her? Charles Abbott replied that this was not the hour for such questions. "The young," she sighed, "are glacial." But that, she proceeded, was exactly what drew her to them. They were like the pure wind along the eaves under which she had been born. "I promise never to kiss you again, or, if I must, solely as the mark of brotherhood. And now go back to——to Andrés."

She backed away from him, superb in the shawl, and again she was rayed in the superlative beauty of her first appearance. The woman was lost in the dancer, the flesh in the vision, the art.

"You could be a goddess," Charles told her, "the shrine of thousands of hearts." The declaration of his entire secret was on his lips; but, after all, it wasn't his. There was a possibility that she had lied about Vincente, and at this second he might be dead, the Volunteers waiting for him, Charles Abbott, below.

*

* *

Hurrying through the Paseo Isabel to the Prado, Charles, looking at his watch, found that it was nearly six. Carmita Escobar and Narcisa, and probably Domingo, were driving perhaps by the sea or perhaps toward Los Molinos, the park of the Captain-General. At any rate the women would be away from the house, and that, in the situation which faced the Escobars, was fortunate. If what La Clavel said were true, and Charles Abbott now believed her implicitly, the agents of the Crown would be already watching in the Prado. Vincente must be smuggled away; how, he didn't yet see; but a consultation would result in a plan for his escape. The servant who opened the small door in the great iron-studded double gate, though he knew Charles Abbott well, was uncommunicative to the point of rudeness. He refused to say who of the family were at home; he intimated that, in any case, Charles would not be seen, and he attempted to close him out.

Charles, however, ignoring the other's protests, forced his way into the arch on the patio. He went up the wide stairs unceremoniously to the suite of formal rooms along the street, where, to his amazement, he found the Escobar family seated in the sombreness of drawn curtains, and all of them with their faces marked with tears. Surprised by his abrupt appearance they showed

[103]

no emotion other than a dull indifference. Then Andrés rose and put his hand on Charles' shoulder, speaking in a level grave voice:

"My dear Abbott, Vincente, our brother, has made the last sacrifice possible to men. He died at noon, sitting in his chair, as a result of the fever."

This was tragic, but, with a deeper knowledge of the dilemma facing them, Charles was actually impatient. "What," he demanded, "are you going to do with the body?"

"It is placed in dignity on a couch, and we have sent to Matanzas for a priest we can trust. He'll be here early in the morning, and then, and then, we must forget our love."

"You must do that now, without a minute's loss," Charles urged them. "You can wait for no priest. The Spanish Government knows he is here; tonight, after dinner, he was to have been taken. The house will be stood on its roof, every inch investigated. You spoke, once, of Narcisa, what might horribly swallow you all. Well, it has almost come."

Andrés' grip tightened; he was pale but quiet. "You are right," he asserted; "but how did you find this out, and save us?" That, Charles replied, was of no importance now. What could

[104]

THE BRIGHT SHAWL

they do with Vincente's body? Carmita, his
mother, began to cry again, noiselessly; Narcisa,
as frigid as a statue in marble, sat with her wide
gaze fastened on Charles Abbott. "What?"
Domingo echoed desperately. It was no longer
a question of the dignity, the blessing, of the
dead, but of the salvation of the living. Vincente's corpse, revered a few minutes before, now
became a hideous menace; it seemed to have
grown to monumental proportions, a thing impossible to put out of sight.

Undoubtedly soldiers were watching, guard-
ing the house: a number of men in nondescript
clothes were lounging persistently under the rows
of Indian laurels below. A hundred practical
objections immediately rose to confront every proposal. Carmita and Narcisa had been sent from
the room, and a discussion was in progress of
the possibility of cutting the body into minute
fragments. "If that is decided on," Domingo
Escobar declared, with sweat rolling over his forehead, "I must do it; my darling and heroic son
would approve; he would wish me to be his
butcher."

Andrés, harder, more mature, than the elder,
stopped such expressions of sentiment. It would
make such a mess, he reminded them; and then,

[105]

how far could the servants, the hysterical negroes, be depended upon? They would soon discover the progress of such an operation.

Charles suggested fire, but the Spanish stoves, with shallow cups for charcoal, were useless, and the ovens were cold; it would create suspicion to set them to burning so late in the day. "Since we can't get rid of it," Charles declared, "we must accept it. The body is there, but whose is it? Did you send a servant to Matanzas?"

Two had gone, riding, once they were beyond Havana, furiously. A Jamaican negro, huge and black, totally unlike Vincente, and a Cuban newly in the city, a mestizo, brought in from the Escobars' small sugar estate near Madriga. Andrés at once appropriated Charles' idea. Their mother and Narcisa, he proclaimed, must go out as usual for their afternoon drive, and he would secure some clothes that belonged to Juan Roman, the servant. No one in the back of the house, luckily, had seen the riders leave. Judged more faithful than the rest, they had been sent away as secretly as possible.

"What," Charles Abbott asked, "caused his death?" Andrés faced him coldly. "This pig of a countryman I killed," he said. "The Spanish will understand that. They have killed a multitude of us, for nothing, for neglect in polishing the back of a boot. It will be more difficult with the servants,—they are used to kindness, consideration, here; but they, too, in other places, have had their lesson. And I was drunk."

In spite of Charles' insistence, he was not permitted to assist in the carrying out of the details that followed. He sat, walked about, alone in the drawing-room. After an interminable wait he heard the report, faint and muffled by walls, of a pistol, and then running feet passed the door. Domingo appeared first, a glass of brandy in his shaking hand:

"He has gone, in a sack, to be thrown into the sea . . . the blood hid his face. Ah, Jesu! But it was successful—a corporal looked, with the hundred doblons I pressed into his hand. He kicked the body three times, thrust a knife into it, and said that there, anyhow, was one less Cuban." Andrés entered the room and, without speech, embraced Charles, kissing him on either cheek; and soon Carmita Escobar and Narcisa, with their parasols and embroidered gloves, returned from their drive.

They could do nothing but wait for what impended, and Charles Abbott related to Andrés the entire scene with La Clavel. "I believe in her," he concluded. Andrés agreed with him. "Her plan is excellent," he pronounced; "it will be very hard on you, though. You will be fed on insults." That, Charles protested, was nothing. "And, worse still, it will end our companionship. You will be able no longer to go about with Jaime and Remigio and me. Yes, that, so soon, is over. What was left of our happiness together has been taken away. We are nothing now in ourselves. How quickly, Charles, we have aged; when I look in the glass I half expect to see grey hair. It is sad, this. Why did you leave your comfort and safety and come to us? But, thank God, you did. It was you who saved us for the present. And that, now, is enough; you must go back to the San Felipe. Put on your best clothes, with a rose in your buttonhole, and get drunk in all the cafés; tell anyone who will listen that La Clavel is more superb than Helen of the Greeks, and buy every Spanish officer you see what he may fancy."

As Charles Abbott left the Escobar dwelling a detachment of Cuban Volunteers on horse, and a file of infantry, their uniform of brown drilling dressed with red collars and cuffs, had gathered across its face. "Quien vive?" a harsh

THE BRIGHT SHAWL

voice stopped him. "Forastero," Charles answered sullenly. He was subjected to a long insolent scrutiny, a whangee cane smote him
sharply across the back. He regarded the men
about him stolidly; while an officer, who had
some English, advised him to keep away from
suspected Cubans. But, at last, he was released,
directed to proceed at once to Anche del Norte
Street, where his passport would be again examined. Charles prepared slowly for dinner at
the Dominica; and, when he was ready to go out,
he was the pattern of a fashionable and idle
young tourist. But what filled his mind was the
speculation whether or not the Escobars would
remember to prevent the return of Juan Roman
with the priest from Matanzas.

*
*   *

Nothing, considering the aspirations of Charles
Abbott, could have been more ironical than the
phase of life he entered upon the acceptance of
La Clavel into the party of independence. The
entire success of this dangerous arrangement depended on his ability to create an impression,
where he was concerned, of unrelieved vapidity.
He was supposed to be infatuated with the dancer;

and he lingered, not wholly sober, about the fashionable resorts. Charles sent her flowers; and, sitting in his room on the roof of the San Felipe, he composed, in a cold distaste, innumerable short variations on the theme of a fluid and fatuous attachment. In reality, he had been repelled by the actuality of La Clavel; he had an unconquerable aversion for her room with its tumbled vivid finery, the powdered scents mingling with the odors of her body and of the brandy always standing in a glass beside her. Yet the discrepancy between the woman herself and the vision she had bred continued to puzzle and disconcert him.

When they were together it was this he preferred to talk about. At times she answered his questioning with a like interest; but all, practically, that she understood about herself, her dancing, had been expressed in their first conversation upon that topic. The rest, at best, was no more than a childlike curiosity and vanity. She had an insatiable appetite for compliment; and, sincere in his admiration for her impersonal aspect, Charles was content to gratify her; except when, in spite of her promise, she kissed him ardently. This never failed to seriously annoy him; and afterwards she would offer him a mock apology. It detracted, he felt, from his dignity, assaulted, insidiously, the elevation of his purpose in life.

He cherished a dislike, part cultivated and part subconscious, for women. All his thoughts and emotions were celibate, chaste. Such a scene had just ended, La Clavel was at her glass, busy with a rouge pot and a scrap of soft leather; and Charles was standing stiffly by the door. She had used, in describing him, a Spanish word about the meaning of which he was not quite clear, but he had an idea that it bore a close resemblance to prig. That specially upset him. At the moment his dislike for her almost broke down his necessary diplomacy. In an island of men desirous of her least favor—her fame transcended seas and reached from coast to coast—he only, thinking less than nothing of his privilege, had an instant unchallenged access to her.

He knew, carefully watched, all her various dependents: Calixto Sola, the hairdresser, a creature with a sterile face constantly twisted into painful grimaces; he was an employee in a barbering shop on Neptune Street, too volatile for any convictions, but because of a spiteful, injured disposition, not to be trusted. Then there was La Clavel's maid, Jobaba, a girl with an

[111]

alabaster beauty indefinitely tainted by Africa. She was, Charles decided, the most corrupt being he had ever encountered. Her life away from the St. Louis was incredibly, wildly, debauched. Among other things, she danced, as the mulata, the rumba, an indescribable affair; and she had connections with the rites of brujeria, the degraded black magic of the Carabale in Cuba. She was beautiful, with a perfection of grace, except for the direct gaze of her brown eyes, which revealed an opacity, a dullness, like mud. She was, even more than to La Clavel, the servant of Santacilla; she reported, the dancer told Charles, every possible act and speech of her mistress to the Spaniards, who, in return, supplied her with a little money and a load of biting curses.

The chambermaid who attended La Clavel's room had lost a lover with the forces of General Agramonte, and was of use to Charles; without knowledge of the hidden actuality she yet brought him, unread, communications for the patriotic party; and she warned him of Santacilla's presence and uncertain humors. The laundress had been, in her youth, an actress in the cheap local theatres, and, when she was not sodden with drink, showed an admirable devotion to her famous patron by the most delicate feats imaginable in ironing. She was almost purely Spanish and had only a contempt for the Cubeños.

While Charles Abbott's duty was, on the surface, direct and easy, it was complicated by the need for a constant watchfulness, a wit in countless small details. Supporting, well enough, the boredom of his public rôle, he had to manage with an unfailing dexterity the transmission of the information that came to the insurrectionists through La Clavel. These facts she gathered through the unguarded moments of Ceaza y Santacilla's talk—he was close to the Captain-General and had important connections at Madrid —and, at prolonged parties, from the conversation of his intimates. Charles put these communications into contracted written English sentences; in that way, even as against the accidental chance of being, at any time, searched, he could better convey their import; and gave them in carefully planned, apparently incidental encounters, to any one of a score of correctly gloved and boutonnièred young men he had come to know by adroitly managed assurances.

Charles had formed, as well, principally in the Café Dominica, a superficial familiarity with

[113]

other Americans in Havana for banking or commercial purposes. They, regarding him as immensely rich and dissipated, were half contemptuous and half eager for the associations, the pleasures, of his mode of life. He went, as often as it seemed necessary, to the United States Club on Virtudes Street, where, together with his patriots, but different from them in a hidden contempt, he gambled, moderately and successfully. His luck became proverbial, and, coupled with La Cavel's name, his reputation soon grew into what he intrigued for. Often, alone on the hotel roof, he regarded himself with an objective amazement: everything was precisely as he had planned, hoped for, on the steamer Morro Castle—and entirely different.

It was probable that the death he had not, in imagination, shrunk from, would crush him at any unexpected moment, an unpredictable slip; but how could he have foreseen the trivial guise he would wear? Charles was forced, it seemed to him, to ape every single quality he hated. The spending of his money, as legitimately as though it were exchanged for guns, on casual acquaintances and rum punches, on gardenias that wilted and entertainment that choked him by its vulgar banality, gradually embittered him. The insincerity of the compliments he paid, the lying compliments to which he listened with an ingenuous smile and an entire comprehension of their worthlessness, steadily robbed his ideal of its radiant aloofness.

His enthusiasm, he discovered, his high ardor, must be changed to patience and fortitude, the qualities which belonged to his temperament and years had to give place to those of an accomplished maturity; the romance of his circumstance deserted the surface to linger hidden, cherished, beneath all the practical and immediate rest. He began to perceive the inescapable disappointing difference between an idea, a conception of the mind, and its execution. The realization of that, he told himself, the seduction of the lofty, the aerial, to earth, constituted success, power. The spirit and the flesh! And the flesh constantly betrayed the highest determinations. How he resented, distrusted, the mechanics, the traps and illusions, of an existence on an animal plane!

His fervor, turned in upon itself, began to assume an aspect of the religious; his imposed revolt from the mundane world turned his thoughts to an intangible heaven, a spotless and immaterial hereafter. The white façades of Havana, intolerably gold under the sun and glimmering in

the tropical nights, the procession and clamor of
the Dia des Reyes, the crowded theatres, the restaurants where, with no appetite, he ate as little
as possible—began to appear vague, unsub-
stantial. What, so intently, was on every hand
being done he thought meaningless. Where, originally, he had been absorbed in bringing relief
to countless specific Cubans, he now only dwelt
on a possible tranquility of souls, a state, like
that promised in the Bible, without corruption
and injustice and tears.

*

*   *

These considerations particularly occupied
Charles Abbott waiting inside the door of Santa
Clara Church for La Clavel, who was coming
to the eight o'clock morning mass. Outside, the
day was still and very hot, intolerably blazing,
but the darkened interior of the church, the air
heavy with incense, was cool. An intermittent
stream of people entered—the white and gilt of
a Spanish naval uniform was followed by gay
silks, a priest passed noiselessly, like a shadow;
an old woman with a rippling fire of jewels made
her way forward, across the wide stone floor, with
the regular subdued tap of a cane. The im-

pending celebration of the mass gathered its activity, its white and black figures, about an altar. Suddenly Charles envied the priests in their service of an ideal embodied in a spiritual Trinity. Even Cuba vanished from the foreground of his thoughts at the conception of a devotion not alone to an island, a nation, but to all the world of men. His interest, measured with this, was merely temporal, limited.

Compared with the Protestant influences of his birth and experience, the separation of religion from society, the all-absorbing gesture and the mysticism of the Roman church offered a complete escape, an obliteration, of the individual. But, as he dwelt upon this, he realized that, for him, it was an impossibility. He might be a Franciscan, begging his way, in brown bagging and sandals, through a callous world for which he ceaselessly prayed; or one of the heroic Jesuits of the early French occupation of the Mississippi Valley. Yet these, as well, were no more than pictures, designs in a kaleidoscope which, immediately turned, would be destroyed in a fresh pattern. He was brought back to reality by the swinging of the heavy curtain at the door; a segment of day, like a white explosion of powder, was visible, and La Clavel proceeded to the font of holy water. As he joined her she complained:

"You should have held it for me in your palm; what barbarians the Americans and English are." She was, characteristically, dressed as brightly as possible, in a mauve skirt with an elaborately cut flounce swaying about yellow silk stockings, a mantón of white crêpe de Chine embroidered with immense emerald green blossoms; her hair piled about its tall comb was covered with a mantilla falling in scallops across her brilliant cheeks. In the church, that reduced so much, she was startling in her bold color and presence.

A negro, whom Charles recognized as a servant at the St. Louis, followed her with a heavy roll and a small unpainted chair with a caned seat. Before the altar, under the low pointed arches of the transept, he spread out a deep-piled Persian rug—where La Clavel promptly kneeled —and set the chair conveniently for her. Her devotion at an end, the dancer rose and disposed herself comfortably. The constant flutter of a fan with sandal wood sticks stirred the edge of her mantilla. After she had scrutinized the worshippers about them, she turned to Charles, speaking in a guarded voice.

He listened with an intense concentration, in

the careful preliminaries of a difficult act of memory, asking her, when it could not be avoided, to repeat facts or names. They were, now, concerned with the New York Junta, involved tables of costs, and La Clavel was palpably annoyed by the unaccustomed necessity of a strict mental effort. She raised her eyebrows, shot an inviting glance at an interested man of middle age, and shut and opened her fan by an irritable twist of the wrist. Watching, weighing, her mood, Charles abruptly brought her recital to an end.

"That is enough for the present," he decided.

"My choice infant," she retorted, "your air of being my director is comic. And I could wish you were not so immaculate, so unworldly—you are tiresome more often than not. I could scream with laughing when I think you are supposed to be my servant of love." The striking of a silvery bell interrupted her with the necessity for a reverence. The mutter of prayer was instantly lost in echoless space. The genuflexions of the priests and acolytes were rapid. "This secrecy," she went on, "is against my disposition, unnatural. I am a woman in whom the complete expression of every feeling is not only a good but a necessity. There are times when I must, it seems, give way to my hatred of those perfumed captains. I sit beside Santacilla, with his hand on my knee, and, hidden by my skirt, my fingers are wedded to the knife in my stocking. A turn, a sweep of the arm . . . there is a tearing cut I learned in the mountains."

The prayers, the Latin invocations, grew louder with the symbolized miracle of transubstantiation, the turning back of the bread and wine into the humility and forbearance of Christ.

Charles Abbott was still, pale and remote; and the heat of La Clavel's words died before the vision of an eternal empire of souls irrevocably judged. She sank forward again, the knotted fringe of her mantón spread out beyond the rug, upon the stone. After a little he told her that her courage, her daring and patience, were magnificent. But she replied that they were cold virtues. "All virtues are cold," Charles assured her seriously. If that were so, La Clavel whispered, her cheek close to his, she was lost to virtue. Anyhow, she didn't believe him, he could not, at his age, know so much. Yet not, God comprehended, that he wasn't both virtuous and cold; any other man in the world, not a heathen, would have flung himself at her. Charles said wearily:

"We have been over this before, and you know

that I do not care for women. What I was a few years ago—"

"A baby," she informed him.

"What I was a few years ago," he repeated with dignity, "is no longer true of me. I belong body and spirit to the cause of which you are aware. And if I didn't it would be, in many respects, no different—science and the liberation of a people are all one, selfless."

"I left the knife out of my present toilet," she sighed. "It would be a charity to free you from the shape you hate so dearly."

"I must go back to the San Felipe and write what you told me," he proceeded. "I understand that Santacilla has gone out on a slaughtering party, and I'll have to take you around in the evening. There are zarzuelas in the Tacon Theatre this evening, and afterwards, I suppose, dulces upstairs at the Tuileries. It's no good, though, expecting me for Retreta—I've got to have some time to recover and sleep: four o'clock last night, with a pack of imbeciles, and three the night before. The smell of Jamaica rum and limes makes me sick."

The mass was over, the people scattering, and, once more cheerful, she laughed at him. "You might wear a hair shirt," she suggested; "they are

[121]

splendid for the soul." He handed her, without reply, into the small victoria, one of the first in Havana, which had taken the place of her volanta. In the sun, her shawl, her smile, were dazzling. A knot of men gathered, gazing at her with longing, regarding Charles Abbott with insolent resentment and wonder; how, their expressions made clear the thought, could that insignificant and colorless foreigner, that tepid American, engage and hold La Clavel, the glory of Cuba and Spain?

She drove away, shielding her eyes with the fan, and Charles returned slowly, on foot, to the hotel, reaching it in time for the eleven o'clock breakfast. Bolting his door, closing the high shutters of his glassless window, he lay down tired and feverish. The vendors of oranges cried, far off, their naranjes, naranjes dulces. The bed, which had no mattress, its sacking covered by a single sheet, the pillow stuffed hard with cotton, offered him little rest. His body, wet with sweat, twisted and turned continually, and sleep evaded him; its peace almost within his grasp, it fled before the hot insistence of his thoughts. The uncomfortable flesh mocked and dragged at the spirit. It occurred to him suddenly, devastatingly, that he might fail in his

[122]

purpose; the armor of his conviction of invincibility fell from him with the semblance of a loud ringing.

*

* *

Of all the disturbing elements in Charles Abbott's present life the one which, it had seemed, must prove most difficult, Santacilla and his friends, troubled him least. There was, in their jeering, a positive quality to be met; his own necessary restraint furnished him with a sustaining feeling of triumph, stability; in his control, the sacrifice of his dignity, his actual pride, damaged by La Clavel, was restored. He acted the part of the infatuated, ubiquitous youth, he thought, with entire success. It had been hardest at first—Santacilla, who pretended to find Charles under his feet like a dog, threatened, if he didn't stay away from the St. Louis, to fling him down the long flight of stairs descending from the dancer's room.

This, Charles wholly realized, was not an idle boasting. Seated, it might be, quietly against the wall, outside the immediate circle about La Clavel, the officers, the Spanish grandees in Cuba for pleasure or for the supervision of their copper mines at Cobra, Charles would watch, study, Ceaza y Santacilla, finding in him the epitome of the Spain he himself hated. What, principally, was evident about the officer with the heavy short neck, the surprising red hair, and small restless blue eyes, was cruelty of an extraordinary refined persistence. He had, unexpectedly in his sheer brutal bulk, a tormenting spirit, a mental abnormality, rather than the to-be-looked-for mere insensate weight of his fist. He was, Charles discovered, the victim of disordered nerves, his gaze, his thick hands or shoulders, were never still, and his lips had a trick of movement as if in the pronunciation of soundless periods.

He spoke, even to La Clavel, abruptly, mockingly; his tenderest words, addressed to her with a sweeping disregard of whoever could overhear, were hasty, introspective rather than generous. More frequently he was silent, redly brooding. It was evident to the most casual understanding that Santacilla was, by birth, association and ideas, an aristocrat of the absolute type fast disappearing. It was his power that, in a world largely affected by the ideal of Christianity, he was ruthless; in an era of comparative humanity he was inhuman. There was, about him, the smell of the slow fires of the Inquisition, of languid murder, curious instruments of pain. Charles recalled a story of the Spanish occupation of Cuba—how the soldiers in armor cut and stabbed their way through a village of naked, unprepared and peaceable bodies.

That, until he had known Santacilla, had been incomprehensible—a page of old history; but now Charles understood: he could see the heavy figure with a darkly suffused face hacking with a sword. He was insane, Charles Abbott told himself; in other circumstances he'd be soon convicted of a sensational murder, quickly hanged or put in an asylum. But in Havana, as an officer of the Crown quartered on a people he held in less esteem than the cattle whose slaughter he applauded in the bull ring, nothing, practically, limited his mad humors. Yes, here, in the West, he was Spain, the old insufferable despotism, and Charles thought of Santacilla's necessary end as coldly as though the soldier were no more than a figment of the doomed old injustice.

La Clavel was seated with Charles Abbott in the upper room of the Tuileries, when Santacilla slid into an unoccupied chair beside them. They were eating mantecados, frozen sweetened cream, and Santacilla dropped a number of battered

Cuban coins, small in denomination, into Charles'
half consumed ice.

"If you were a man," he said, "you could
break them up with your teeth."

The other quietly put the plate away and
lighted a cigarette. He smiled, as if in appreciation of his humor, at the officer.

"But I'll bet you twenty doblons you can't break
one," he added.

Santacilla replied that he was considering
having Charles Abbott deported.

"You are so dangerous," he explained, with
the grimace that served him as a smile. "I
often consult with our Captain-General. 'This
Abbott,' he says; 'Agramonte is nothing, but I
am afraid of him. He is wise, he is deep.' And
then we think what can be done with you—a tap
on the head, not too hard and not far from the
ear, would make you as gentle as a kitten. I
have had it done; really it is a favor, since then
you would forget all your trouble, the problems
of state. You'd cry if I raised a finger at you."
La Clavel interrupted him to swear at his degraded imagination. "And the figure in the
jota!" he turned to her. "You know that the
Spaniards of birth have, as well as their own,
the blood of the Moriscos. What they were,

[126]

what the East is, with women, I beg you to remember.

"This new treatment of women is very regret-
table. I am a little late for absolute happiness;
too late, for example, to fasten your tongue with
a copper wire to the tongue across the table from
you. Lovers, you see, joined at last." He
talked while he ate, in a manner wholly delicate,
minute fragile dulces, cakes, glazed in green and
pink, and ornamental confections of almond
paste. Unperturbed, La Cavel found him com-
parable to a number of appalling objects and
states. Coarse, was all that he replied.

"You are a peasant, a beast, and what you say
is merely stupid. There this Abbott is your superior—he has a trace, a suspicion, of blood. I
am wondering," he was addressing Charles again.
"It seems impossible that you are as dull as you
appear; there is more, perhaps, than meets the
eye. Your friendship with the Escobars broke
up very suddenly; and you never see Florez and
Quintara with his borrowed French airs. They
are nothing, it is true, yet they have a little Castilian, they are better than the avaricious fools at
the United States Club. Of course, if you are in
love with this cow gone mad, a great deal is ac-
counted for." He wiped his fingers first on a

THE BRIGHT SHAWL

serviette and then on a sheer web of linen marked
with a coronet and his cipher.

"Pah!" he exclaimed, looking at the dancer,
"your neck is dirty again."

Sick with disgust, his blood racing with a passionate detestation, Charles Abbott laughed
loudly. But he was relieved that Santacilla's
attention had been shifted from him. Another
officer, a major of the Isabel regiment, tall and
dark and melancholy, joined them. He ignored
Charles completely, and talked to La Clavel about
her dances—the Arragonese jota and those of the
other provinces of Spain. He had, it developed,
written an opera on the subject of de Gama and
a fabulous Florida. Santacilla grew restive at
this and gazed about the room maliciously.
Then, suddenly, he rose and walked to the table
where a young Cuban exquisite was sitting with
a girl slender and darkly lovely. Santacilla
leaned over, with his hands planted on their
table, and made a remark that drove the blood in
a scarlet tide to the civilian's face. Then the
Spaniard amazingly produced from his sleeve a
ball of lamb's wool such as women use to powder
their faces, and touched the girl's nose lightly.
He went to another table and repeated his act,
to another and another, brushing all the femi-

nine noses, and returned, unchallenged, to his place.

"If I had been with any of those women," he related comfortably, "and the King had done that, there would have been a new king and a new infanta."

The musical Spaniard, inappropriately in uniform, remonstrated, "A lot of them will kill you some night in the Paseo de Valdez or on the quays."

Santacilla agreed with him. "No doubt it will overtake me—if not here, then on the Peninsula. A hundred deaths, all distressing, have been sworn upon me." Charles Abbott's expression was inane, but, correcting that statement, he said to himself, "A hundred and one."

La Clavel yawned, opening to their fullest extent her lips on superb teeth and a healthy throat.

"I have, at least, a sponge, a basin of water," she proclaimed indirectly.

Santacilla replied, "You think nothing can cleanse me, and, in your chattering way, you are right; except, it may be, that last twist of steel or ounce of lead. Some of my soldiers are planning to manage it; I know them well, and I gave one an opportunity today: I stood with my back to him in the parapet of the Twelve Apostles for

three, five, minutes, while he tramped and fiddled
with his musket, and then I put him in a hole in
the stone for a year."

*

*   *

.The other Spanish officer, Gaspar Arco de
Vaca, Santacilla's closest companion, observed toward Charles an air of profound civility, and his
pretence was more galling than Santacilla's mor-
bid threats and exposed contempt.   De Vaca was,
in temperament and appearance, purely Iberian:
he was of middle height, he carried his slender
body with an assured insulting grace, and had a
narrow high-boned face, a bigoted nose and a
moustache like a scrolling of India ink on a re-
pressed and secretive mouth.   Charles often encountered him in the Fencing School on the Prado,
across from the Villa Nueva Theatre.   The officers of Isabella congregated there late in the
afternoon, where they occupied all the chairs and
filled the bare room with the soft stamp of their
heels and the harsh grinding of engaged buttoned
steel.   The foils, however, were not always covered: there had been some fatalities from duel-
ling in the sala de Armas since Charles Abbott had
been in Havana; a Cuban gentleman past sixty

[130]

had been slain by a subaltern of seventeen; two officers, quarreling over a crillo girl, had sustained punctured lungs, from which one had bled to death.

The Cubans, it was made evident, were there by sufferance, and the fencing master, Galope Hormiguero, an officer who had been retired from a Castilian regiment under the shadow cf an unprovoked murder, made little effort to conceal his disdain of the Islanders. Charles he regarded without interest: he was a faithful student, and made all the required passes, engaged the other beginning students, with regularity; but even he saw that he would never be notably skilful with the foil or rapier or broadsword. Charles had a delicate sense of touch, he bore himself firmly, his eye was true; he had the appearance of mastery, but the essence of it was not in him. His heart, Hormiguero frequently told him, was like a sponge; he wasn't tempered to the commanding of death.

He agreed, silently, that he wasn't a butcher; and as for his heart—time would show its material. Meanwhile he kept up the waist and forearm exercises, the indicated breathing, gaining, if not a different spirit, a harder and cured body. The room was large, with the usual high windows on a balcony, and strips of coco-matting over the tiled floor. A light wooden partition provided dressing space, the chairs were carried about hither and there, and the racks of foils against the walls reflected the brightness of day in sudden long shivers like other and immaterial blades. It had been, originally, a drawing-room, the cornice was elaborate, and painted on the ceiling were flying cupids and azure and cornucopias of spilling flowers.

At moments of rest, his chest laboring and arms limp at his sides, Charles Abbott would stare up at the remote pastoral of love and Venus and roses. Then the clamor, the wicked scrape of steel, the sharp breaths, the sibilant cries that accompanied the lunges, would appear wholly incomprehensible to him, a business in a mad-house; he'd want to tear the plastron, with its scarlet heart sewn high on the left, from his chest, and fling it, with his gauntlet and mask, across the floor; he'd want to break all the foils, and banish Galope Hormiguero to live among the wild beasts he resembled. He was deep in such a mood when de Vaca's considerate tones roused him. "Positively," he said, "you are like one of the heroes who held Mexico on the point of his sword or who swept the coast of Peru of its gold. And you are idle, for you see no one who can hold the mat with you."

"In reality," Charles replied, "I fence very awkwardly. But you have often seen me, I haven't any need to tell you that."

"That can never be established without experience," the Spaniard asserted; "I should have to feel your wrist against mine. If you will be patient, if you will wait for me, I'll risk a public humiliation."

Charles Abbott said evenly: "I'd be very glad to fence with you, of course."

When de Vaca, flawlessly appointed, returned, Charles rose steadily, and strapped on his mask, tightened the leather of the plastron. A murmur of subdued amusement followed their walking out together onto an unoccupied strip—de Vaca was a celebrated swordsman. Charles saluted acceptably, but the wielding of the other's gesture of courtesy filled him with admiration. The foils struck together, there was a conventional pass and parry, and from that moment Charles Abbott lost control of his steel. At a touch from de Vaca, scarcely perceptible, his foil rose or fell, swept to one side or the other; a lunge would end in the button describing a whole arc, and pointing either to the matting or the

[133]

winged and cherubic cupids. The laughter from the chairs grew louder, more unguarded, and then settled into a constant stream of applause and merriment.

Disengaged, he said in tones which he tried in vain to make steady, "You have a beautiful hand."

De Vaca, his eyes shining blackly through wire mesh, thanked him in the politest language known. He began, then, to make points, touches, wherever he chose—with a remarkably timed twist he tore the cloth heart from Charles' wadding; he indicated, as though he were a teacher with a pointer, anatomical facts and regions; de Vaca seemed to be calling Charles' attention, by sharp premonitory taps, to what he might have been saying. There were now a number of voices encouraging and applauding him; he was begged not to be so hard upon Gaspar; and it was hoped that he was not giving way to the venting of a secret spite. A nerveless parry in tierce brought out a tempestuous support—

His arm was as heavy, as numb, as lead, the conventional period had been ignored, and his torment went on and on. His chest, he thought, must burst under the strapped plastron, and sweat poured in a sheet across his eyes. The episode seemed utterly meaningless, undemanded; the more remarkable because of de Vaca's indifference to him, to all the trivialities of his Cuban duty. How yellow the face was, the eyes were like jet, through the mask. Then Charles Abbott grasped what, he was certain, was the purpose of such an apparently disproportionate attack. It was the result of a cold effort, a set determination, to destroy what courage he had. He gazed quickly about, and saw nothing but Spanish faces; the fencing master was in the far end of the room, intent upon a sheaf of foils. At any moment de Vaca could have disarmed him, sent his steel flying through air; but that he forebore to do. Instead he opposed his skill, his finesse, his strength, in the attack upon Charles Abbott's fibre.

"If I collapse," Charles told himself, "it will be for eternity."

Any sense of time was disintegrated in a physical agony which required all his wasting being to combat. But, even worse that that, far more destructive, was the assault upon his mind. If he crumbled . . . he thought of himself as dust, his brain a dry powder in his skull. The laughter around him, which had seemed to retreat farther and farther, had ceased, as though it had been lost in the distance. The room, widening to an immensity of space, was silent, charged with a malignant expectancy. Soon, Charles felt, he would fall into unreckoned depths of corrupt shadows, among the obscene figures of the hideously lost.

The sweat streaming into his mouth turned thick and salt—blood, from his nose. There was a tumult in his head: his fencing now was the mere waving of a reed. Again and again the Spaniard's foil, as cruelly and vitally direct as at the first pass, struck within Charles' guard. The face of wood, of yellow wood, the eyes that were bits of coal, behind the mask, pursued him into the back of his brain. It stirred, there, a smothering instinct, a dormant memory, and Charles, with a wrenching effort, in a voice thin like a trickle of water from a spigot, said again, "—a most beautiful hand."

Sharply, incomprehensibly, it was over. Drooping forward upon his knees, dropping his foil from paralysed fingers, he saw de Vaca, with his mask on an arm, frowning.

"Now," Charles Abbott thought luxuriously, "I can faint and be damned to them."

The cloud of darkness which flowed over him was empty of the vileness of fear; rather, like the

[136]

beneficence of night, it was an utterly peaceful remission of the flesh.

*

*   *

His physical exhaustion, the weariness of his mind, continued in a settled lassitude through the following day. He was to see Andrés Escobar, give him what information he had had from La Clavel, the next morning at the baths of the Campos Eliseos; and meanwhile he scarcely stirred from the San Felipe. Charles, for the time, lacked the bravado necessary for the sustaining of his pretence. His thoughts, turned in upon his own acts and prospects, dwelt quietly on his determination. He had changed appreciably during his stay in Havana; even his physiognomy was different—how, he couldn't say, but he was aware that his expression had, well, hardened. The cure which had been the principally hoped-for result of Cuba was complete. In spite of his collapse in the fencing school, he was more compactly strong than ever before. It occurred to him that, now, he might be described as a man.

This brought him a certain pleasure, and, in keeping with that state, he tried to simplify, to comprehend, the idealism which dominated him. He didn't want to grasp vainly at rosy clouds.

[137]

His first attitude, one of hardly more than boy-ish excitement, had soon become a deep imper-sonal engagement—he had promised himself to Cuba. That will was stronger than ever; but the schooling of the past weeks, together with the stiffening of his spirit, had bred a new practical-ity in him, superior, he felt, to any sheer heroics. He vastly preferred the latter, he hadn't totally lost the inspiring mental picture of a glorious sacrifice; but he had come to the realization that it was more important to stay alive. What, in reality, he was trying to do was to see himself consecutively, logically.

In this, he recognized, his mind was differ-ent from the Escobars', from the blind fervor of the many Cuban patriots he knew. He could see that reflected in their manner toward him: no trace of Vincente's aloofness remained, they had come, forgetting his comparative youth, his alien blood, to regard him with almost an anxiety of re-spect. When it was possible, men of the widest possible activities talked to him of their plans. In short, Charles Abbott felt that he might be-come a power; and this he coolly set himself to bring about. His heritage was that of success; there were distinguished men, who had carried alone heavy responsibilities to their justified end, no more than two or three generations behind him. His mother, he thought gladly, surveying her in the clearness of a full detachment, had an astonishing courage of spirit. Charles told himself that he would have to become a politician; his undiminished idealism, without which his validity was nothing, must be shut into his heart, held purely for the communication of its force and for his own benefit.

The simple path of truth, of partisan enthusiasm, must be put aside. The uncalculating bravery of the men gathered about General Agramonte was of indispensable value; but undirected, with no brain to make secure, to put into operation, the fire they created, that would come to little. He wished that his connection, his duty, with La Clavel was over, that he could delegate it elsewhere, but, obviously, for the moment, that was impossible. It merely remained for him, then, to take no unpondered chances, never again to be drawn into such a situation as he had faced with Gaspar Arco de Vaca.

Before such a sharp decision, a certain amount of his sheer joy evaporated: it was less inspiring to be cautious than daring. The Cubans themselves, always excepting Andrés, had lost an appreciable amount of their glamour for him.

[139]

They were, now, units, elements, to be managed, to be tranquilized, steadied, moved about. All this, of course, was yet to come; the recognition of him was instinctive rather than acknowledged. But, he repeated to himself, it was forming, spreading. That, then, was the shape, the actuality, of his vision—to establish himself indispensably at the fore of a Cuban liberty, incipient, dreamed of, and accomplished. All his thoughts dropped, almost with the audible smooth clicking of meshed steel gears, into place. The last degree of joy was replaced by a fresh calm maturity. He would never, it was obvious, be a leader of soldiers, and he had no desire to become the visible head of government; no, his intention was other than that of Carlos de Cespedes. He viewed his future self rather as a powerful source of advice with a house on the Prado. It was curious how coldly, exactly, he planned so much; and he stopped to examine his ambition even more closely and to discover if it were merely absurd.

It struck him that it might be he had lost too much, that already he had become selfish, ambitious for himself, and he recalled the religious aspect so quickly gone. No, he decided, his effort was to bridge that space, already recognized, between desire and realization. Anyhow, he determined to speak of this as well to Andrés during their bath. The April temporale lay in an even heat over the city, and the end of the Paseo Isabel was crowded by the quitrins of women, the caleseros, in their brilliant livery, sleeping in whatever shade offered. The Escobars had a private bath, but Andrés preferred the larger baño publico, where it was possible to swim, and there Charles found him. The basin had been hollowed from the coral rock; it was perhaps eighteen or twenty feet square, and the height of the water, with a passage for a fresh circulation cut in the front wall, was level with the calm reach of the sea.

The pool, as clear as slightly congealed and cooled air, open to the horizon, was roofed, with a railed ledge and steps descending into the water, and Andrés Escobar sat with his legs half immersed. He greeted Charles conventionally, concealing the pleasure which shone in his eyes.

"I stopped at your dressing-room," Charles Abbott told him; "anything might be taken from the pockets of your coat."

The converse of this possibility, that something had been put into a pocket, he conveyed. Andrés nodded indifferently. The other slid into the water, sinking and swimming beneath the surface to the farther end. It was delicious. Swimming was his only finished active accomplishment; and, with a half concealed pride, he exhibited it in skilful variations. Even the public bath, he felt, was too contracted for the full expression of his ability. In addition to this, it was necessary to talk confidentially to Andrés. And so, with a wave of his arm, he indicated the freedom of the sea beyond.

Andrés Escobar followed him over the stone barrier, and together they swam steadily out into the blue. Finally, they rested, floating, and Charles diffidently related what was in his heart. His friend, less secure in the water, listened with a gravity occasionally marred by a mouthful of sea.

"You are right," he agreed, when Charles had finished. "Although you have put it modestly, I think—many of us admit—that you may be a strong man in Cuba. Indeed, I have heard it said that you should go back to America, and put more intensity into the Junta. Naturally I should regret that, but we must all do what, in the end, is best. Charles, there is a great deal of water under and around us, and I should feel better nearer the Campos Eliseos."

"Wait," Charles Abbott replied with a touch of impatience; "you are quite safe, there is no tide at present." Floating in the calm immensity, his arms outspread, his face, at once burned by the sun and lapped by water, turned to the opposed azure above, he drew in accession after accession of a determination like peace. Nothing should upset what he had planned. There was a stir beside him—André Escobar was returning to the shore, and lazily, thoughtfully, he swam back. The Cuban left immediately, for breakfast; but Charles lingered in the pool, lounging upon the wooden grilling with a cigarette. One by one the bathers went away. The sky, the sea, were a blaze of blue. The clatter of hoofs, the caleseros' departing cries, sounded from the Paseo. "Charles Abbott," he repeated his own name aloud with an accent of surprise. What, whom, did it describe? He gazed down over his drying body. This, then, was he—the two legs, thin but sufficiently muscular, the trunk in a swimming suit, the arms and hands! His hidden brain, his invisible mind, was himself as well; and, of the two, the mind and the body, the unseen was overwhelmingly the more important. He remembered how, fencing with de Vaca, the body had failed him utterly; de Vaca, attacking

[143]

his will, was contemptuous of the other . . . and
his will had survived. Rising, he felt that he
commanded himself absolutely; he had no sympathy, no patience, for frailty, for a failure
through the celebrated weaknesses of humanity:
hardness was the indispensable trait of success.

*

*   *

The whole of reasonably intelligent life,
Charles discovered, was disrupted by the ceaseless
clash of two utterly opposed ideas, emotions.
There was, first, the need in the individual to
serve, to justify, himself, to maintain his integrity; and, as well, there was the duty—at least, it
was universally called a duty—of a self-sacrifice
for love. The failures of superior men came
largely, he was certain, in the breaking down of
the first through the second. A man, for example,
put into motion the accomplishment of his own
demand, and then was appalled by the incidental
price, but more to others than to himself. Yes,
love betrayed men. The Escobars were, insep-
arably, Cuba, they were happily merged, lost,
in one supreme cause; yet the superiority of their
hearts over the head endangered their dearest preoccupation. They saw symbols as realities, they

[144]

wrongly valued emotion more highly than reasoning.

And further, Charles returned to himself, if he had consulted and listened to his parents, if his love of home had outweighed his singular vision, he would be nothing now but an unimportant drifting figure. His parents had had more knowledge of life than he; undoubtedly their counsel, in the main, was correct, safe. That word, safe, was it specially. The instinct of his mother was to preserve, to spare, him; to win for him as smooth a passage through life as was procurable. She had her particular feminine idea of what, in her son, spelled solid accomplishment; and, with all her spirit, it was material in so far as it was visible: position in a settled community, the money necessary for an existence both dignified and ornamental, a "nice" wife—another devoted sheltering soul such as herself—and well-behaved handsome children. The inner qualities she demanded for him were faith, honesty, and fidelity.

Her vision of a broad close-cut lawn and grey stone house with pillars and a port-cochère, his wife, in silks and chaste jewels, receiving a polite company in the drawing-room, was admirable. In it he would be gray-haired and, together with an increasing stoutness, of an assured dignity. His children would worship his wisdom and paternal benevolence, and the world of affairs would listen to him with attentive respect. It was, unquestionably, an impressive conception. Every detail was excellent, but he cared for, revered, none of them.

He didn't want to be safe, to decline softly to a soft old age, a death smothered in feathers. More than anything else his desire was to live intensely, to ride, upright, the crest of a thunderous wave. He hated, now, every phase of a decent suburban smugness. Someone else was welcome to the girl designated, by his mother, to be his wife. Someone other than himself might sit across the dinner-table from her, week after week, month after month, year after year, and watch her stereotyped face beyond the cut flowers; another might listen to the interminable gabble about servants and neighbors and dresses and cards. The children would be differently, more appropriately, fathered; his, Charles Abbott's, potential children were gathered into an ideal that was, too, an idea. It must be served, realized, within the dimensions of his own bone and fibre; it was exclusively his, his the danger, the penalty and the reward. Charles would not have had it different, even if, although none existed, he had any choice.

He must, however, prepare himself against the betrayal he was able to trace so clearly in others; there could be no faltering, no remorse; he was cut off from the ordinary solaces, the comfortable compactness, of general living. But, already, temperamentally, he liked, preferred, this; alone, never for a minute was he lonely. The inattention to home, primarily the result of a new scene and of exciting circumstances, had grown into an impersonal fondness for his family; he failed to miss them, to wish for their presence. The only element that remained from the past was his love for Andrés Escobar; he confronted it valorously, deposed it from his mind, but it clung around his heart. How fortunate it was that Andrés could not detach him from his resolve; it was unthinkable that one should stand in the way of the other.

These reflections occupied his mind at various times and places: one day in the American Consulate on Obispo Street; again at the steamship office on Mercaderes; over his cigarette and cheese and jelly at the Noble Havana; strolling along Ricla Street where the principal shops were congregated; at a dinner party in the Palace of

[147]

the Conde de Santovernia. He was aloof. All the activity that absorbed the people among whom he went was to him trivial, utterly of no consequence. Sometimes he would walk through the stalls of the Mercado de Cristina, on the Plaza Vieja, or in through the Honradez factory on Sol Street, where a handful of cigars was courteously given to any appreciative visitor. He would return along the Paseo de Valdez to the park where he had sat when he was first in Cuba, and, as then, the strains of the military band of the Cabañas drifted across the bay.

The dwelling of the Captain-General, with the Royal Lottery on the ground floor, had before it sentries in red and white; the Quay de Caballería, reached through the Plaza of San Francisco, was tempered and pleasant in the early dusk, and at the Quay de Machina was a small garden with grotesque rosy flamingoes and gold-fish in the fountain. He sat, as well, lonely, considering and content, in the Alameda de Paula, where, by the glorieta, it was called the Salon O'Donnell. The moats, filled with earth, truck gardens, the shore covered with sugar pans, engaged his absent-minded interest. With the improvement of his Spanish, he deserted the better known cafés and restaurants, the insolence of the Cas-

THE BRIGHT SHAWL

tilian officers, for modest Cuban places of food, where he drank Catalan wine, and smoked the Vegueros, the rough excellent plantation cigars.

This new mood, he was relieved to find, gave his acquaintances as much amusement as his public dissipation—it was ascribed to the predicted collapse of his love affair with La Clavel. She was, he was rallied, growing tired of his attentions; and, in the United States Club, he was requested not to drown himself, because of the trouble it would cause his country. Captain Santacilla, however, studied him with a growing ill-humor; his peculiar threats and small brutalities had stopped, but his temper, Charles recognized, was becoming dangerous. He declared frankly, in the Café Dominica, that Charles wasn't the fool he appeared, and he repeated his assertions of the need for a deportation or worse.

This was a condition which, sooner or later, must be met, and for which Charles prepared himself. Both Cubans and Spaniards occasionally disappeared forever—the former summarily shot by a file of muskets in a fosse, and the latter, straying in the anonymous paths of dissipation, quieted by a patriotic or vindictive knife. This, it seemed to Charles Abbott, would be the wisest plan with Santacilla; and he had another strange

[149]

view of himself considering and plotting a murder. The officer, who had an extraordinary sense of intangible surrounding feelings and pressures, spoke again to Charles of the efforts to dispose of him.

"The man doesn't draw breath who will do it," he proclaimed to Charles, at the entrance to the Valla de Gallo. "It's a superstition, but I'd back it with my last onza of gold. I've seen it in you very lately, but give it up. Or don't give it up. Either way you are unimportant. I can't understand why you are still here, why I permit you to live. If I remember it I'll speak to my sergeant, Javier Gua: he performs such an errand to a nicety. I have taken a dislike to you, very unreasonably, for you are no more than a camarone. I believe, for all your appearance of money, that La Clavel supports you; it is her doblons, I am certain, you gamble away and spend for food."

Charles Abbott smiled at the insult:

"On one hand I hear that she has thrown me over and then you say that she supports me. Which, I wonder, is to be preferred? But neither, fortunately, is true. I can still buy her a bouquet of camellias and she will still wear it. As for the money, I never lose at gambling, Santacilla, I am always successful; the cards are in my favor. If I bet on the black, it turns up; and when I choose the red, affairs are red."

Santacilla's uneasy eyes shifted over him suspiciously. "Blood and death, that is what black and red are," he said. "But you are not the dispenser of fate." The peak of his cockaded hat threw a shadow over his sanguine face to the chin. "A camarone," he repeated, "a stalk of celery. Gua, and I'll remember to tell him, will part you from your conceit." There was a metallic crowing of roosters as the officer turned away.

*

*   *

La Clavel noticed a marked difference in Charles, but proclaimed that it was no more than an increase in his natural propensity for high-mindedness. It fatigued her, she declared, to be with him, made her dizzy to gaze up at his altitude of mind. He was seated in her room, the hair-dresser was sweating in the attempt to produce an effect she was describing to him with phrases as stinging as the whip of foils, while Charles watched her with a degree of annoyance. Her humors, where he was concerned, were unpredictable; and lately she had found a special delight in attacks on his dignity. She said and did things—an air of innocence hiding her malice —indecently ribald that shook his firmest efforts to appear, to be, unconcerned.

At last, in a volatile rage, she dismissed the servant with his tongs and pomatum and crimping leads, and swore to Charles Abbott that she was going to the Argentine by the first boat that offered passage.

"I am sick of Cuba, and I've forgotten that I am an artist, and that is bad. You are wrapped up in this liberty, and that is very well for you, an ordinary person. You must have something like that, outside you, to follow, for you've very little within. But me, I am not an ordinary person; I am La Clavel. I am more valuable to the world than pumpkins or republics. I stamp my heel," she stamped her heel, a clear sharp sound, and her body swept into a line passionate and tense, "and I create a people, a history." La Clavel secured the castanets lying on her dressing-table—in answer to their irritable rhythmic clinking she projected, for an instant, a vision of all desire.

"I can make men forget; I can draw them out of their sorrows and away from their homes; I can put fever in their blood that will blind them to memories and duty. Or I can be a drum, and lead them out, without a regret, a fear, to death. That is more than a naranjada or a cigar or an election. And, because of what I have given you, I have put that out of my life; I have been living like the mistress of a bodega. To be clear, Charles, I am tired of you and Cuba, and I have satisfied my hatred of the officers with cologne on their handkerchiefs."

"I understand that perfectly," Charles Abbott assured her; "and I cannot beg you to stay. Whatever your motive was, your value to us has been beyond any payment. If our movement had a saint, you would fill that place."

She laughed, "A strange saint in a mantón and slippers with painted heels."

"Much better, Charles replied, "than many of those in sanctified robes. I had the feeling, too," he proceeded, "that our usefulness together was coming to an end." It seemed to him that again she had become the glorified figure of the stage, his dislike for her actuality, her flesh, vanished, leaving only profound admiration.

"I am amazed," she said, in a lingering half humorous resentment, "that you never loved me, I never brought you a regret or a longing or made any trouble in your heart."

[153]

"That was because I put you so high," he explained. She raised her shoulders and objected that it was late for compliments.

"Be honest—you didn't care for me. You ought to be very successful, you have things surprising in the so young. Will you," she demanded suddenly, totally changing the subject, "be my maid?" He hastened to inform her, vehemently, that he would not. "Jobaba hasn't come today," La Clavel continued; "and she wasn't here to dress me for dinner last evening. That is unusual in her: I have a feeling she is not coming back."

"Perhaps she has been murdered in one of the brujos cabildos," Charles suggested. "It is impossible to say where that frenzy stops." A happening quite different, the dancer told him, was in her mind.

"I could never get into the thoughts of Jobaba," she admitted. "And there is very little I miss. I suppose it's the negro. She is like cream, smooth and beautiful to look at, but turned by thunder." If she were going away, Charles reminded her, there were a number of things to be discussed and closed. And she told Charles how a Cuban, ostensibly attached to the national party, but in reality a Spanish secret

[154]

agent, had been sent into Camagüey.   His name
was Rimblas.

Charles Abbott repeated that, and memorized
such characteristics as La Clavel knew.   There
was an indefinite stir at the door, a short knock,
and he moved to the window as Santacilla entered
unceremoniously.

The Spaniard was a model of politeness, of
consideration, and he listened, seated with his
hands folded about the head of his officer's cane,
to La Clavel's determination to go to South
America.   It was an excellent plan, he agreed;
they would welcome her rapturously in Buenos
Aires; but hadn't she put off her intention a little
too long?   It was on account of the climate, the
season, he hastened to add.   Although, of course,
they would open the opera house for her,
the smart world would come in from their es-
tancias.

"But what will our young American do?" he
demanded.   "How will he live without his delight?   But perhaps he is going to the Argentine
with you.   He will have a busy time, and a hat-
ful of challenges there, where beauty is appre-
ciated to the full."

Charles said, with an appearance of sullen-
ness, that he hadn't been invited to go farther

[155]

south; and Santacilla replied that, as a matter of fact, it might be necessary for him to remain, perhaps forever, in Havana. He spoke cheerfully, gazing amiably upon them, but a vague quality of his bearing, his voice, was disturbing, mocking. His words had the air of an underlying meaning different from their sound. An uneasiness, as well, was communicated to La Clavel: she watched Santacilla with an indirect puzzled gaze.

"Jobaba has gone," she announced abruptly.

The trace of a smile hovered about the officer's expression of regret. "A personable clip of hell," was his opinion of the strayed maid. "Do you remember the major who composed music?" he addressed La Clavel. "Well, he was always a little touched in the brain, and he caught this negro hysteria, he became a brujos. He'd come home in the morning with his body marked in yellow chalk, and wrung out like a boatman's sponge; and he let drop a fact or two about your Jobaba screaming to an African drum rubbed with the fingers. In that state, he said, a great deal that was curious and valuable could be dragged from her. We encouraged his madness, at the Cabañas, for what it brought us. But it was unfortunate for him—he ties bright rags

about his ankles and mumbles, when he thinks
he is alone."

Charles Abbott's mind, sifting all that the other
said, was abnormally active, sharp. Something,
he couldn't quite grasp what, was acutely, threat-
eningly, wrong. He had a sense of impending
danger, a premonition of clashing sound, of dis-
cord. And, whatever developed, he must meet
it, subdue and conquer it. Ceaza y Santacilla,
he saw, was not visibly armed; but, probably, he
would carry a small pistol. The one his father
had given him was in Charles' pocket. The difficulty was that, in the event of a disturbance, no
matter what the outcome here might happen to
be, the dancer and he would bear the weight of
any Spanish fury. And it was no part of his
intention to be cut in half by bullets behind a
fortress wall.

He could only delay, discover as soon as possible what was behind Santacilla's deceiving patience and good humor. Upon that he would
have to act without hesitation and with no chance
of failure. The regiment should, the dancer complained, send her maid back to her. Manners
were very much corrupted beyond the western
ocean—in Sevilla the servant would have been
dispatched in a bullock cart deep in roses. That,

he answered, reminded him of another procession, a different cart; but it was more French than Castilian—the tumbril.

He was seated against a wall at a right angle from the door, and Charles left the vicinity of the window, lounging across the room. La Clavel said, "I know you so well, Ceaza, what is it; what is it you are saying and saying without speaking of? Your mind is like a locked metal box that shows only the flashes on the surface. But you must open it for us. It seems as though you were threatening me, and that, you best should realize, is useless."

His flickering eyes rested first on her and then upon Charles Abbott. "You will never get to South America now," he asserted; "for you are a conspirator against your King. Since you have shown such a love of Cuban soil you are to become a part of it forever."

*

*   *

Charles Abbott, now standing by the door, shot in the bolt which secured it, and, by a fortunate, a chance, twist, broke off the handle. Santacilla, undisturbed, remained seated, smiling while his fingers played with the plaited loop of his cane.

[158]

"This infatuation," he indicated them with a wave, "while it convinced Havana, never entirely satisfied me. I have been watching you, Jobaba has been listening, for days. You were very cunning, but, in the end, you failed; you were neither skilful nor patient enough. Yet, at the last, all that you heard were fairy tales—the spy that was sent to Camagüey, ha!"

La Clavel faced him calmly, but, Charles saw, she was pale. He was revolving a hundred impractical schemes: they had only one end, the death of Santacilla, but how that was to be brought about with safety to Cuba evaded him.

"I am not a traitor in the way you mean," she declared; "what your conceit never allowed you to note was that, in Spain and here, I have always detested you; and what I did was the result of that. I struck at you and not at our country, for the court and church and army are no longer our strength—if we still have any except the knife and cord—but our weakness.

"Fools," he asserted, unmoved.

"And now you are the fool," she added.

"No, you are wrong; I am only enjoying myself before the show is over. I wanted to see you, and your young devotee, twist and turn before the fact of death. I have killed, and seen executed, a number of people, men and women; but I was still curious—a great dancer and a rich young American. That is an unusual day."

It was best, Charles Abbott decided, to bring about as much as possible with no more delay; the prime necessary act accomplished, they could face the problems of the immediate future steadily. He quietly produced his pistol and levelled it. The dry click which alone followed the pulling of the trigger made the officer aware of the attempt upon his life. A dark angry surge invaded his face, and then receded. "No man will ever kill me," he repeated. "It is my star." A hand left the cane and produced a small gold whistle.

Charles stared dully at the useless weapon, with its mounting of mother-of-pearl, which he still held.

"The cartridges have been too long in their barrels," Santacilla explained; "they have dried and shifted. You should have greased them every week."

La Clavel stood, lost in thought, like a woman in a dream. Her hair, over which she had spent such time and curses, was an elaborate silhouette against the light. "Ceaza, Ceaza," she implored, going to him, "you must let me go

[160]

and dance in Buenos Aires, they have never seen
me there, it is necessary to my career." She was
close beside him, when he rose suddenly, pushing
the chair between them.

"You Andalusian devil!" he cried, and put
the whistle to his lips. Before he could blow,
the dancer had flung herself on him, with an arm
bound about his neck, a hand dragging at his
throat. The whistle fell, the chair was brushed
aside, and the man and woman, in a straining
desperate grip, swayed into the middle of the
floor.

Charles, driven by an inherited instinct to pro-
tect La Clavel, to replace her in such a struggle,
caught at either of the locked shoulders; but,
whirling in the passion of their strife, they struck
him aside. He made another effort to pull Santacilla to the floor, without success; and then,
with a small stout chair in his hands, he waited
for an opportunity to bring it crashing on the
officer's head. He was appalled by the fury of
the woman silently trying to choke her enemy;
her other hand, grasping the thin glimmer of the
knife always convenient in her stocking, the
officer held away from them. Her years of dancing, her early hardening life in the mountains,
had given her a strength and litheness now tear-

ing at the weight, the masculinity, of Santacilla. He was trying, in vain, to break her wrist, to close his fingers into her throat; and, bending, the fragility of her clothes ripped across her sinuous back. Shifting and evading the thrust of his power, she was sending the blood in purple waves over his neck and thick cheeks. Neither of them cried out, spoke; there was only the sound of hoarse breathing, inarticulate expressions of unendurable strain. Charles Abbott, raising, holding poised, the chair, and lowering it, was choked with the grappling horror before him.

La Clavel's face was as blanched as the officer's was dark, her eyes were wide-open and set, as though she were in a galvanic trance. Again and again Santacilla tried to tear away her arms, to release himself from the constriction at his neck. His fingers dug red furrows through her flesh, they tormented and outraged her. A palm closed upon her countenance, and blood ran from under it. But there was no weakening of her force, no slackening in her superb body. She seemed curiously impersonal; robbed of all traits of women; she was like a symbolical fate, the figure from a shield, from an emblem, dragging him to death.

Then, suddenly, in an inadequate muffled

voice burdened with a shuddering echo of fear, he cried for her to release him. It was so unexpected, he became so inexplicably limp, that La Clavel backed away instinctively. Charles started forward, the chair lifted high; but he was stopped by the expression, the color, of Ceazy Santacilla's face. The officer turned, with his hands at his throat, toward the window. He took an uncertain step, and then stood wavering, strangely helpless, pathetically stricken.

"The air," he whispered; "hot as wine." He pitched abruptly face forward upon the floor.

La Clavel tried to speak against the labored heaving of her breast, but what she attempted to say was unintelligible. Charles, slipping back the broken bolt with a finger in its orifice, listened intently at the door. The Hotel St. Louis was wrapped undisturbed in its siesta; no alarm had been created. Santacilla lay as he had fallen, an arm loosely outspread, a leg doubled unnaturally under its fellow. He bore the laxness, the emptiness, of death. He had spoken truly that it wasn't in his star to be killed by a man. Finding that he was still holding the chair, Charles put it softly down. "Well," he said, "the revolution is through with him."

He glanced suddenly at La Clavel. She was

drooping, disheveled and hideous; her hair lay on her bare shoulders in coarse strands; her face was swollen with bruises. Now, he realized, she would never see the Argentine; she would never again hear the shouted olés that greeted, rewarded, the brilliancy of her jota. His thoughts shifted to Cuba and himself—if it were a crime of passion that had been committed in her room, the cause, there, would be freed from suspicion. He had, as customary, come directly, unostentatiously, to her room, and he was certain that he had not been observed. A duty, hard in the extreme, was before him.

"Why did you bring about Santacilla's death?" he demanded. She gazed at him dully, uncomprehendingly. "It was because he was jealous," he proceeded; "you must hold to that." She nodded, dazed. "When they come into the room and find him you must show what he did to you. And, after all, you didn't kill him. Perhaps that will save you," his voice was without conviction. "They won't believe you, and they may try measures to get at the truth; but you will be faithful. You will keep your secret, and—and I must go. I shall ask for you downstairs, make them send up a servant, and shout as loudly as any."

THE BRIGHT SHAWL

She held up her battered countenance dumbly and, with a feeling of transcendent reverence, he kissed her cut lips. Thrown across the end of the bed, the shawl she had danced in, blazing with gay color, cast the reflection of its carmines and yellows on the calcimined wall. It was like a burst of the music which accompanied her dancing. The castanets lay on the floor. The blessed saint of Cuban independence! Then the caution that had become a part of his necessity rode uppermost: he proceeded silently to the door, and, closing it behind him, went, meeting no one, to the ground floor, where he pulled irritably at the wire hanging from a bell under the ceiling. The raw jangle brought a servant, a rosy-cheeked Gallego boy, heavy with sleep, who went stumbling up the stairs on Charles' errand.

*

*   *

In his own room a wave of physical horror swept over Charles Abbott; he was obliged to sit down, and the chair, the floor, seemed to rock at the giddy sickness of the memory of Santacilla, stumbling with a wine-colored face toward the window in a vain gasping for air, for life. He recovered slowly: notwithstanding the

[165]

death of Tirso Labrador, the wasted shape of Andrés' brother, all the tragedies he had heard reported, it was not until now that he realized the entire grimness of the undertaking against Spain. The last possibility of the spectacular departed, leaving him with a new sense of the imminence of death. He had considered this, under certain circumstances welcoming it, or dismissing it with a creditable calmness, many times before; but then his attitude had been softened by the detachment, the impersonality, of his view. But at last the feeling of death was tangibly at his own throat; not today, nor tomorrow, probably; but inescapably. Well, he assured himself, he wouldn't, at that intense moment, fail an inner necessity; but his understanding gave him an additional feeling of the accidental aspects of life and of the Cuban revolution.

Until then he had, sub-consciously, except for one short depression, been certain of the ultimate triumph of right; he had thought it must succeed through its mere rightness; and he had pictured justice as a condition dropped beneficently from the clouds, wrought with the thunder of angels' wings. But accomplishment on earth, with men, he now saw, was neither safe, easy nor assured. It was the result of bitter struggle, a strife open to the most appalling mischances. A necessity of the spirit, it must be executed in the flesh, and flesh was a treacherous, unstable substance; it was capable not only of traitorous betrayals, but equally of honest, and no less fatal, failures. With this in his thoughts he went to the door, in answer to a knock, and received a heavy carefully tied parcel.

He opened it, and, dripping in dazzling color from the wrapping paper, was La Clavel's mantón, the one in which he had first seen her insolently dancing the jota. Charles, with a stirred heart, searched carefully for a note, a scrap of revealing paper; but there was none. She had sent it to him silently, before she had been taken away, in a sentiment the delicacy of which deeply moved him. He laid the shawl over the bed, where its cruel brilliancy filled the white-walled room, darkened against the heat, with flashes of magenta and orange and burning blue. La Clavel had worn it dancing, where it emphasized her grace and perversity and stark passion; it had been, in Charles Abbott's mind, synonymous with her, with the vision she created; but, suddenly, it lost that significance, and he saw it as the revealed outspread pattern of his own existence.

THE BRIGHT SHAWL

The shawl was a map, a representation, of the country of the spirit through which he passed; such emotions, such heat, and such golden roses, all had been, were, his against that background of perilous endeavor. It seemed to float up from the bed and to reach from coast to coast, from end to end, of Cuba; its flowers took root and grew, casting about splendor and perfume; the blue widened into the sky, the tenderness of the clasping sea; the dark greens were the shadows of the great ceiba trees, the gloom of the jungles, the massed royal palms of the plains. And not only was it the setting, the country, its violent dissonances became cries, victorious or hopeless, the sweep of reddened swords, the explosions of muskets. There was the blood that had welled into the Laurel Ditch of Cabañas; and, as well, the sultry mysterious presence of Africa in the West—the buzzing madness of the music of the danzón, the hysterics of brujeria.

Charles, at the heart of this, stood enveloped, surrounded, by a drama like the sharp clash of cymbals. It was easy to be overwhelmed, strangled, blinded, by the savage color; briefly to be obliterated. That possibility had been, lately, very much in his mind; and he wondered, against all his recent change, if, in the surrender of his idealism, he had lost his amulet, his safety. While he had, to a large extent, solved, for himself, the philosophy of conduct, cleared the motives of his acts, a great deal was inexplicable still. He saw, dimly, that there could be little hope of justice on any island except as the projection, the replica, of a fundamental universal integrity of justice. Perfection like that couldn't begin on the rim of being and extend inward; it must be at the center of all life, obscured, delayed, but, in an end not computable in the span of human existence, certain and inevitable. Charles Abbott now had the feeling that, parallel with the maintaining of his grasp on materialism, his recognition of the means at his hand, there should be an allegiance to a supremacy of the immeasurable whole.

That double vision, the acceptance of a general good together with the possibility of extreme ill to the individual, puzzled him. He was required to put faith in a power seemingly indifferent to him, to discharge a responsibility in return for which nothing that he could weigh was promised. Charles recalled what had overtaken the dancer, La Clavel, in payment for a heroic effort against an insupportable oppression. Disaster had met the body, the flesh; what occurred

[169]

in the spirit he was unable to grasp; but this, suddenly, breathlessly, he saw:

La Clavel's bitter defiance, her mountain-born hatred of oppression, her beaten but undefiled body, had communicated to him something of her own valor. It was as though she had given him a palm, a shielded flame, to add to his own fortitude. In all probability she would, soon, be dead; Charles correctly gauged the Spanish animosity; and yet she was alive, strong, in him. She would be living; it was Ceaza y Santacilla who had died, been vanquished; his abnormal refinement dropping so easily into the bestial, the measure of evil, in him, for which he stood, had been slain, dissipated, ended. The shawl contracted, became a thing magnificent but silk, a mantón invested with a significance brave and suprisingly tender. It was, now, the standard of La Clavel, the mantle of the saintliness he had proclaimed. His doubts, his questioning, were resolved into the conviction that the act of the dancer was her spirit made visible, created tangibly for a tangible purpose, and that, there, she was indestructible.

With that conclusion to serve as a stay and a belief, a philosophy of conduct, he returned from the extra-mundane to the world. Charles thought of La Clavel's desire to dance in Buenos Aires, for South America. He wondered how old she was; he had never before considered her in any connection with age; she had seemed neither old nor young, but as invested with the timeless quality of her art. She had spoken often of her girlhood, but no picture of her as a girl had formed in his mind. It was conceivable that, in more stable circumstances, she would have grown old, become withered with the peculiar ugliness of aged Spanish women; but that, too, he could not realize. Somehow, La Clavel's being was her dancing, and what had gone before, or what might have followed, were irrelevant, unreal; they were not she. He understood, now, her protest against being absorbed, involved, in anything but her profession.

He became conscious of the sustained gravity of his thoughts, how his activity had been forced from the body to his mind; and that recalled to him the necessity for a contrary appearance. It would be wise for him to go to the Café Dominica that evening, in an obvious facile excitement at his connection, at once close and remote, with the death of Santacilla in the dancer's room. But, beyond the fact that it was known he had dispatched the servant up-stairs, and the usual wild,

thin speculations, nothing had been allowed to
appear. Santacilla, it was announced, had died
naturally. La Clavel wasn't mentioned. She
had spoken to others than Charles of her determination to go to the Argentine; and it was probable, rumor said, principally in Spanish mouths,
that she would go quietly south. At the United
States Club, the idlers and gamblers surveyed
Charles with dubious looks; and, over a rum
punch, he adopted a sullen uncommunicative air.
It would not do to drop his widely advertised
habits too suddenly; he could not, in a day,
change from a rake to a serious student of such
books as Machiavelli's Prince; and he prepared,
with utter disgust, for his final bow in the cloak
of dissipation.

*

* *

Purely by accident he met, at the Plaza de
Toros, Jaime Quintara, Remigio Florez and
Andrés. It was so fortunately, evidently, hap-
hazard, that they continued together while Charles
related the circumstances of the tragedy in La
Clavel's room. The others were filled with wonder, bravos, at her strength and courage. Some-
day, Remigio swore, when Cuba was free, he

would put up a monument to her in India Park. It would be of heroic size, the bronze figure of a dancer, in a mantón, on a block of stone, with an appropriate inscription.

"The trouble with that," Andrés objected, "is if we should live and put up a monument to everyone who deserved it, the parks would be too crowded with bronzes for walking. All of Cuba might have to be commemorated in metal."

At Neptuno Street and the Paseo Isabel they parted. Charles proceeded alone toward the sea; and, with the knowledge that Andrés had not gone home, but would be evident in public elsewhere, he stopped to see the other members of the Escobar family. Carmita Escobar had faded perceptibly since Vincente's death; still riven by sorrow she ceaselessly regretted the unhappy, the blasphemous, necessity which made the wearing of mourning for him inadmissible. Domingo Escobar, as well, showed the effects of continuous strain; his vein of humor was exhausted, he no longer provoked Charles' inadequate Spanish; he avoided any direct reference to Cuba. He was, he said, considering moving to Paris, he was getting old and no one could complain, now, since—. He broke off, evidently at the point of referring to Vincente and the Escobar local patriotism.

[173]

But Narcisa, Charles was told, had become promised to Hector Carmache, an admirable gentleman with large sugar interests; luckily, for Narcisa, unconnected with any political dreams.

"She will be very happy," her mother proclaimed.

Narcisa narrowed her eyes. "He lives on an estancia," she added, "where there will be banana trees and Haitians to watch; and the conversation will be about the number of arrobas the mill grinds." She relapsed again into silence; but, from her lowered countenance, he caught a quick significant glance toward the balcony. She rose, presently, and walked out. Charles gazed at Domingo and Carmita Escobar; they were sunk in thought, inattentive, and he quietly joined Narcisa.

"Andrés has told me a great deal about you," she proceeded; "I made him. He loves you too, and he says that you are very strong and respected everywhere. I have had to hear it like that, for you never come here now. And I hear other things, too, but from my maid, about the dancer, La Clavel. You gamble, it seems, and drink as well."

That, he replied, was no more than half true; it was often necessary for him to appear other

[174]

than he was. He studied her at length: she had grown more lovely, positively beautiful, in the past month; the maturity of her engagement to marry had already intensified her. Narcisa's skirt had been lowered and her hair, which had hung like a black fan, was tied with a ribbon.

"How do you like me?" she demanded. But when he told her very much, she shook her head in denial. "I ought to be ashamed," she added, "but I am not. Did you realize that, when we were out here before, I made you a proposal? You ignored it, of course. . . . I am not ashamed of what I did then, either. Afterwards, standing here, I wanted to throw myself to the street; but, you see, I hadn't the courage. It's better now, that time has gone—I'll get fat and frightful."

"This Carmache," Charles Abbott asked, "don't you like, no, love him?" She answered: "He is, perhaps, fifty—I am fifteen—and quite deaf on one side, I can never remember which; and he smells like bagasse. I've only seen him once, for a minute, alone, and then he wanted me to sit on his knees. I said if he made me I'd kill him some night when he was asleep. But he only laughed and tried to catch me. You should have heard him breathing; he couldn't. He called me his Carmencita. But, I suppose, I shall come to forget that, as well. I wanted you to know all about it; so, when you hear of my marriage, you will understand what to look for."

"That is all very wrong!" Charles exclaimed.

In reply she said, hurriedly, "Kiss me."

That was wrong, too, he repeated, afterward. Her warmth and tender fragrance clung to him like the touch of flower petals. She turned away, standing at the front of the balcony, her arms, bare under elbow ruffles, resting on the railing. The flambeau trees in the Parque Isabel were like conflagrations. Her head drooped on her slender neck until it almost rested, despairingly, on the support before her. "I hate your northern way of living," her voice was suppressed, disturbingly mature; "I hate their bringing you into the house, only to break my heart. Charles," she laid an appealing hand on his sleeve, "could you do this—help me to run away? We have cousins in New York who would receive me. If you could just get me on a steamer!"

"No," he said decidedly, "I could not; I wouldn't even if it were possible. What would Andrés, my friend, think? It would ruin me here."

"If you had," she admitted, after a little, "as

[176]

soon as we reached the street, I would have locked myself about your neck like my crystal beads. Once when I was supposed to be going with a servant to the sea baths, I had the quitrin stop at the San Felipe, and I went up the stair, to the roof, to your room, but you were out. You see, I am a very evil girl."

He agreed to the extent that she was a very foolish girl. In turn she studied him carefully.

"You seem to have no heart," she announced finally; "not because you don't love me, but in affairs generally; but I can tell you a secret— you have! It's as plain as water. What you think you are—poof!" She blew across the open palm of her hand.

"I hope not," he returned anxiously. "But you are too young, even if you are to be married, to know about or to discuss such things. As An- drés' best friend I must caution you—"

"Why did you kiss me?" she interrupted.

He was, now, genuinely sorry that he had, but he replied that it had been no more than the sa- lute of a brother. "You had better go in," he con- tinued; "when they realize we are out here there will be a stir, perhaps you will be put to bed."

"I might make a scandal," she deliberated, "throw myself on you and cry as loudly as possible." A smile appeared upon her fresh charming lips at his expression of dismay. "Then you would have to marry me."

"I'd have to spank you," he retorted.

"I shall never speak directly to you again," she concluded; "so you must remember what I say, that you are not what you'd like to be."

She was, he thought, in spite of her loveliness, a very disagreeable little girl. That designation, ludicrously inadequate, he forced upon himself. With a flutter of her skirts she was gone. The afternoon was so still that he could hear the drilling of soldiers by the shore, the faint guttural commands and the concerted grounding of muskets. Narcisa and her unpleasant prediction faded from his mind. Standing on the balcony he imagined a vast concourse gathered below with upturned faces, waiting for him to speak. He heard the round periods, the sonorous Spanish, he delivered, welcoming, in the name of the people, their newly gained independence, and extending to them the applause and reassurances of the United States.

"You have won this for yourselves," he proclaimed, "by your valor and faith and patience; and no alien, myself least of all, could have been indispensable to you. What I was privileged to do was merely to hold together some of the more inglorious but necessary parts of your struggle; to bring, perhaps, some understanding, some good will, from the world outside. You have added Cuba to the invaluable, the priceless, parts of the earth where men are free; a deed wrought by the sacrifice of the best among you. Liberty, as always, is watered by blood—" he hesitated, frowning, something was wrong about that last phrase, of, yes—the watered with blood part; sprinkled, nourished, given birth in? That last was the correct, the inevitable, form. The hollow disembodied voice of the drill sergeant floated up and then was lost in the beginning afternoon procession of carriages.

*

*   *

With a larger boutonnière than he would have cared to wear at home, a tea rose, he was making his way through the El Louvre, when Gaspar Arco de Vaca rose from a gay table and signalled for him. It was after Retreta, the trade wind was even more refreshing than customary, and the spirit of Havana, in the parques and paseos and restaurants, was high. The Louvre was

[179]

crowded, a dense mass of feminine color against the white linen of the men, and an animated chatter, like the bubbles of champagne made articulate, eddied about the tables laden with dulces and the cold sweet brightness of ices. He hesitated, but de Vaca was insistent, and Charles approached the table.

"If you think you can remain by yourself," the Spaniard said pleasantly, "you are mistaken. For women now, because of the dancer, you are a figure of enormous interest."

He presented Charles to a petulant woman with a long nose, a seductive mouth, and black hair low in the French manner; then to a small woman in a dinner dress everywhere glittering with clear glass beads, and eyes in which, as he gazed briefly into them, Charles found bottomless wells of interrogation and promise. He met a girl to whom, then, he paid little attention, and a man past middle age with cropped grey hair on a uniformly brown head and the gilt floriations of a general. A place was made for Charles into which, against his intention, he was forced by a light insistence. It was, he discovered, beside the girl; and, because of their proximity, he turned to her.

At once he recognized that she was unusual,

strange: he had dismissed her as plain, if not actually ugly, and that judgment he was forced to recall. The truth was that she possessed a rare fascination; but where, exactly, did it lie? She was, he thought, even younger than Narcisa, yet, at the same time, she had the balanced calm of absolute maturity. Then he realized that a large part of her enigmatic charm came from the fact that she was, to a marked degree, Chinese. Her face, evenly, opaquely, pale, was flat, an oval which held eyes with full, ivory-like lids, narrow eye brows, a straight small nose and lips heavily coated with a carmine that failed utterly to disguise their level strength. Her lustreless hair, which might have been soot metamorphosed into straight broad strands, was drawn back severely, without ornament or visible pins, over her shapely skull. She wore no jewelry, no gold bands nor rings nor pendants; and her dress, cut squarely open at her slim round throat, was the fragile essence of virginity. She attracted Charles, although he could think of nothing in the world to say to her; he was powerless to imagine what interested her; a girl, she had no flavor of the conceits of her years; feminine, she was without the slightest indication of appropriate sentiments, little facile interests or enthusiasms.

[181]

From time to time she looked at him, he caught a glimpse of eyes, blue, grey or green, oblique and disturbing; she said nothing and ate in infinitesimal amounts the frozen concoction of sapote before her.

Charles Abbott hadn't grasped her name, and in reply to his further query, she told him in a low voice that it was Pilar, Pilar de Lima. Yes, she had been born in Peru. No, she had never been to China, although she had travelled as far as Portugal and London. His interest in her increased, she was so wholly outside his— any conceivable—life; and, without words, in a manner which defied his analysis, she managed to convey to him the assurance that he was not impossible to her.

He found, at intervals, fresh qualities to engage him: she had unmistakably the ease which came from the command of money; the pointed grace of her hands—for an instant her palm had sought his—hid an unexpected firmness; she was contemptuous of the other vivacious women at the table; and not a change of expression crossed the placidity of a countenance no more than a mask for what, mysterious and not placid, was back of it. Then, in an undertone during a burst of conversation, she said, "I like you." She was

[182]

half turned from him, in profile, and her lips
had not seemed to move. Seen that way her
nose was minute, the upward twist of her eye
emphasized, her mouth no more than a painted
sardonic curl. She was as slender as a boy of a
race unknown to Charles—without warmth, without impulses, fashioned delicately for rooms
hung in peacock silks and courtyards of fretted
alabaster and burnished cedar.

He wanted to reply that he liked her, but, in
prospect, that seemed awkward, banal; and a
lull in the conversation discouraged him. Instead he examined his feelings in regard to this
Pilar from Lima. It was obvious that she had
nothing in common with the women he had dismissed from his present and future; she was
more detached, even, than La Clavel on the stage.
And when, abruptly, she began to talk to him, in
an even flow of incomprehensible vowels and sib-
ilants, he was startled. Gaspar de Vaca spoke
to her in a peremptory tone, and then he addressed Charles, "She'll hardly say a word in a
Christian tongue, but, when it suits her, she
will sail on in Chinese for a quarter of an hour.
It may be her sense of humor, it may be a prayer,
perhaps what she says, if it could be understood,
would blast your brain, and perhaps she merely

has a stomach ache." But his remonstrance had the effect designed; and after an imperturable silence, she said again that she liked Charles Abbott.

The General regretfully pushed back his chair, rose, and held out an arm in formal gallantry, and Charles was left to follow with Pilar. She lingered, while the others went on, and asked him if, tomorrow, he would take her driving to Los Molinos. He hesitated, uncertain of the wisdom of such a proceeding, when her hand again stole into his. What, anyhow, in the face of that direct request, could he do but agree? They must have, she proceeded, since he hadn't a private equipage, the newest quitrin he could procure, and a calesero more brilliant than any they should pass on the Calzada de la Reina. After all he would be but keeping up the useful pretence of his worldliness; yet, looking forward to the drive with her, an hour in the scented shade of the Captain-General's gardens, he was aware of an anticipated pleasure.

The need for caution was reduced to a minimum, it shrank from existence; naturally he wouldn't talk to Pilar de Lima of politics, he could not be drawn into the mention of his friends, of any names connected in the slightest way with a national independence. It was possible that she had been selected, thrown with him, for that very purpose; but there his intelligence, he thought, his knowledge of intrigue, had been underestimated, insulted. No—Pilar, de Vaca, Spain, would gain nothing, and he would have a very pleasant, an oddly stimulating and exciting, afternoon. The excitement came from her extraordinary personality, an intensity tempered with a remoteness, an indifference, which he specially enjoyed after the last few tempestuous days. Being with her resembled floating in a barge on a fabulous Celestial river between banks of high green bamboo. It had no ulterior significance. She was positively inhuman.

He met her, with an impressive glittering carriage and rider, according to her appointment, at the end of the Paseo Tacon, past the heat of afternoon. She was accompanied by a duenna with rustling silk on a tall gaunt frame, and a harsh countenance, the upper lip marred by a bluish shadow, swathed in a heavy black mantilla. Pilar was exactly the same as she had been the evening before. The diminished but still bright day showed no flaw on the evenness of her pallor, the artificial carmine of her lips was like the applied petals of a geranium, her narrow sexless body was upright in its film of clear white.

[185]

THE BRIGHT SHAWL

The older woman was assisted into the leather body of the quitrin, Pilar settled lightly in the niña bonita, Charles mounted to the third place, the calesero swung up on the horse outside the shafts, and they rattled smartly into the Queen's Drive. From where he sat he could see nothing but the sombre edge of the mantilla beside him and Pilar's erect back, her long slim neck which gave her head, her densely arranged hair, an appearance of too great weight. On either side the fountains and glorietas, the files of close-planted laurel trees, whirled behind them. The statue of Carlos III gave way to the Jardin Botánico.

*

*   *

There he commanded the carriage to halt, and, in reply to Pilar's surprise, explained that he was following the established course. "We leave the quitrin here, and it meets us at the gates of the Quinta, and meanwhile we walk. There are a great many paths and flowers." On the ground she admitted her ignorance of Havana, and, followed at a conventional distance by her companion, they entered the Gardens. There was a warm perfumed steam of watered blossoming

[186]

plants and exotic trees; and Charles chose a way that brought them into an avenue of palms, through which the fading sunlight fell in diagonal bands, to a wide stone basin where water lilies spread their curd-like whiteness. There they paused, and Pilar sat on the edge of the pool, with one hand dipping in the water. He saw that, remarkably, she resembled a water lily bloom, she was as still, as densely pale; and he told her this in his best manner. But if it pleased her he was unable to discover. A hundred feet away from them the chaperone cast her replica on the unstirred surface of the water, in the middle of which a fountain of shells maintained a cool splashing.

"I should like one of those," she said, indicating a floating flower.

"It's too far out," he responded, and she turned her slow scrutiny upon him. Her eyes were neither blue nor gray but green, the green of a stone.

"That you are agreeable is more important than you know," she said deliberately. "And de Vaca—" she conveyed a sense of disdain. "What is it that he wants so much from you? How can it, on this little island, a place with only two cities, be important? I must tell you that I

[187]

am not cheap; and when I was brought here, to see a boy, it annoyed me. But I am annoyed no longer," her wet fingers swiftly left their prints on his cheek. "Oporto and the English Court—I understood that; but to dig secrets from you, an innocent young American," she relapsed into silence as though he, the subject she had introduced, were insufficient to excuse the clatter of speech. So far as he was concerned, he replied, he had no idea of her meaning.

"You see," he went on more volubly, "I was, to some extent, connected with the death of Santacilla, an officer of the regiment of Isabel, and they may still be looking for information about that."

She assured him he was wrong. "It is Cuba that troubles them. It's in their heads you are close to powerful families here and in North America, and that you are bringing them together, pouring Northern gold into the empty pockets of the Revolution. I saw at once, before I met you, that I should waste my time, and I was going away at once . . . until you walked into the restaurant. Now it will amuse me, and I shall take the doblons I get and buy you a present, a ruby, and, when you see Captain de Vaca, you will wear it and smile and he will know nothing."

"You mustn't buy me anything," Charles protested earnestly; "I can at least understand that, how generous you are. If you are unfamiliar with Cuba perhaps you will let me inform you. I came to Havana, you see, for my lungs. They were bad, and now they are good; and that is my history here. There is no hole in them because I have been careful to avoid the troubles on the street; and the way to miss them is not to give them an admission. The reason I am here with you is because you seemed to me, in yourself, so far away from all that. Your mind might be in China." He went on to make clear to her his distrust of women. "But you are different; you are like a statue that has come to life, a very lovely statue. What you really are doesn't matter, I don't care, I shall never know. But a water lily—that is enough."

"Are you wise or no deeper than this?" she asked, indicating the shallow fountain. "But don't answer; how, as you say, can it affect us? You are you and I am I. We might even love each other with no more; that would be best— it is the more that spoils love."

"What do you know about that?"

But, relapsing into immobility, she ignored his question. Beyond doubt his interest in her had increased; it was an attraction without name, yet none the less potent. Seated close beside him she still seemed to be fashioned from a vital material other than flesh and blood; she was like a creation of sheer magic . . . for what end? They rose, leaving the Botanical Gardens, the spotted orchids and air plants and oleanders, for the Quinta. There they passed into a walk completely arched over with the bushes of the Mar Pacifico, the rose of the Pacific, a verdurous tunnel of leaves and broad fragrant pink blooms, with a farther glimpse of a cascade over mossy rocks.

The stream entered a canal, holding some gaily painted and cushioned row boats, and a green-gold flotilla of Mandarin ducks. There were aviaries of doves, about which strollers were gathered, and a distant somnolent military guard. It was the first time for weeks that Charles had been consciously relaxed, submerged in an unguarded pleasure of being. Pilar might be honest about de Vaca and his purpose, or she might be covering something infinitely more cunning. It would bring her nothing! The very simplicity of his relationship with her was a complete protection; he had no impulse to be serious, nothing in his conversation to guard.

THE BRIGHT SHAWL

Pilar seemed singuarly young here, engaged in staring at and fingering the flowers, reading the sign boards that designated the various pleasances —the Wood of the Princess, the Garden of San Antonio, the Queen's Glade. Her tactile curiosity was insatiable, she trailed her sensitive hands over every strange surface that offered. Then, with her airy skirt momentarily caught on a spear of bearded grass, he saw, below her knee, under the white stocking, the impression of a blade, narrow and wicked. La Clavel had carried a knife in that manner, many women, he had no doubt, did; but in Pilar its stealthy subdued gleam affected him unpleasantly. It presented a sharp mocking contrast to all that, in connection with her, had been running happily through his mind.

"I thought you were a moth, soft and white," he told her; "but it appears that you are a wasp in disguise—I hope it won't occur to you to sting me."

Serenely she resettled her skirt. "Did you look for a scapular? Young men's eyes should be on the sky." Then she put an arm through his. "It was never there for you . . . a moth soft and white. But I don't care for that." Her gliding magnetic touch again passed, like the fall

[191]

of a leaf, over his cheek. Affecting not to notice it he lighted a thin cigar; he'd have to watch Pilar de Lima. Or was it himself who needed care? The feeling of detachment, of security, was pierced by a more acute emotion, a sensation that resembled the traced point of her knife. She asked, nearing the place where they were to meet the quitrin, when she might see him again; and mechanically he suggested that evening, after the music in the Plaza de Armas.

Returning to Ancha del Norte Street, his face was grave, almost concerned, but he was made happy by finding Andrés Escobar in his room. Andrés, with the window shades lowered, was lounging and smoking in his fine cambric shirt sleeves. He had a business of routine to communicate, and then he listened, censoriously, to Charles' account of his afternoon.

"She is a little devil, of course, with her gartered steel, but she amuses me. I have the shadow of an idea that she was truthful about de Vaca; and the ruby would be an excellent joke."

"I cannot approve of any of this," Andrés decided; "it has so many hidden possibilities—the Spaniards are so hellish cunning. To be candid with you, I can't understand why they have neg-

[192]

lected you so long. You are, Charles, fairly conspicuous. Perhaps it is because they hope, in the end, to get information from you. In that case, if we were in danger, I would shoot you with my own hand. Drop this Chinese water lily; their stems are always in the mud."

"On the contrary, you must see her," Charles Abbott insisted. "I've explained that she can't hurt us; and we may get something floated the other way." He was aware of an indefinable resentment at Andrés' attitude: his love for him was all that prevented the acerbity of a voiced irritation.

*

*   *

Yet, when the regimental band was leaving to the diminishing strains of its quickstep, Andrés joined Charles and Pilar—who had left her quitrin—strolling through the Plaza. As usual she said practically nothing; but, in the gloom, she was specially potent, like a fascinating and ironic idol to innocence; and Charles Abbott was pleased by Andrés' instant attention. Pilar was reluctant, now, to return to the carriage, and she lingered between the men, who, in turn, gazed down addressing remarks to the smooth blackness of

[193]

her hair or to the immobile whiteness of her face. Charles dropped behind, to light a cigar, and when he came up to them again he had the illusive sense of a rapid speech stopped at his approach. Andrés Escobar's countenance was lowered, his brow drawn together . . . it had been Pilar de Lima, surprisingly, who had talked. Charles recalled the manner in which her low, even voice flowed from scarcely moving lips, with never a shadow of emotion, of animation, across her unstirred flattened features.

Some Cubans gathered about the table when, later, they were eating ices; and, gaining Pilar's consent, he left with the indispensable polite regrets and bows. He was vaguely and thoroughly disturbed, uneasy, as though a grain of poison had entered him and were circulating through all his being. It was a condition he was unfamiliar with, disagreeable in the extreme; and one which he determined to stamp out. It hadn't existed in his contact with Pilar until the appearance of Andrés; yes, it came about from the conjunction of the girl, Andrés and himself; spilled into the clarity of their companionship, Andrés and his, her influence had already darkened and slightly embittered it . . . had affected it, Charles added; she was powerless to touch him

[194]

in the future; he put her resolutely, completely, from his thoughts.

He was a little appalled at the suddenness with which the poison had tainted him, infecting every quality of superiority, of detachment, of reasoning, he possessed. When he saw Andrés again, after the interval of a week, his heart was empty of everything but crystal admiration, affection; but Andrés was obscured, his bearing even defiant. They were at a reception given by a connection of the Cespedes on the Cerro. Instinctively they had drawn aside, behind a screen of pomegranate and mignonette trees in the patio; but their privacy, Charles felt, had been uncomfortably invaded. He spoke of this, gravely, and Andrés suddenly drooped in extreme dejection.

"Why did you ever bring us together!" he exclaimed. "She, Pilar, has fastened herself about me like one of those pale strangling orchids. No other woman alive could have troubled me, but, then, Pilar is not a woman." Charles Abbott explained his agreement with that.

"What is she?" Andrés cried. "She says nothing, she hardly ever lifts her eyes from her hands, I can give you my word kissing her is like tasting a sherbet; and yet I can't put her out of my mind. I get all my thoughts, my feelings, from her as though they passed in a body from her brain to mine. They are thoughts I detest. Charles, when I am away from you, I doubt and question you, and sink into an indifference toward all we are, all we have been."

"Something like that began to happen to me," Charles admitted; "it was necessary to bring it to an end; just as you must. Such things are not for us. Drop her, Andrés, on the Paseo, where she belongs." The other again slipped outside the bounds of their friendship. "I must ask you to make no such allusion," he retorted stiffly. Charles laughed, "You old idiot," he said affectionately, "have her and get over it, then, as soon as possible; I won't argue with you about such affairs, that's plain." Andrés laid a gripping hand on his arm, avoiding, while he spoke, Charles' searching gaze.

"There is one thing you can do for me," he hurried on, "and—and I beg you not to refuse. The mantón that belonged to La Clavel! I described it to Pilar, and she is mad to wear it to the danzón at the Tacon Theatre. You see, it was embroidered by the Chinese, and it is appropriate for her. Think of Pilar in that shawl, Charles."

THE BRIGHT SHAWL

"She can't have it," he answered shortly.

Andrés Escobar's face darkened. "It had occurred to me you might refuse," he replied.
"Then there is nothing for me to do. But it
surprises me, when I remember the circumstances,
that you have such a tender feeling for it. After
all, it wasn't a souvenir of love; you never lost
an opportunity to say how worn you were with
La Clavel."

"No, Andrés, it isn't a token of love, but a ban-
ner, yours even more than mine, a charge we must
keep above the earth."

That, Andrés observed satirically, was very
pretty; but a mantón, a woman's thing, had no
relation to the cause of Cuban independence.

"Perhaps, but of course, you are right," Charles
agreed. "Very well, then it is only a superstition of mine. I have the feeling that if we lower
this—this standard it will bring us bad luck, it
will be disastrous. What that Pilar, you may
think, is to you, the mantón has always been for
me. It is in my blood; I regard it as a sailor
might a chart. And then, Andrés, remember—it
protected Cuba."

"I have to have it," the other whispered
desperately; "she—she wants it, for the danzón."

[197]

Charles Abbott's resentment changed to pity, and then to a calm acceptance of what had the aspect of undeviating fate. "Very well," he said quietly. "After all, you are right, it is nothing but a shawl, and our love for each other must not suffer. I'll give it to you freely, Andrés: she will look wonderful in it."

The other grasped his hands. "Be patient, Charles," he begged. "This will go and leave us as we were before, as we shall always be. It hasn't touched what you know of, it is absolutely aside from that—a little scene in front of the curtain between the acts of the serious, the main, piece. I doubted her honesty, as you described it, at first; but you were right. She has no interest at all in our small struggle; she is only anxious to return to Peru."

"I wish she had never come from there!" Charles declared; "whether she is honest or dishonest is unimportant. She is spoiled, like a bad lime."

"If you had been more successful with her—" Andrés paused significantly.

"So that," Charles returned, "is what she said or hinted to you!" Andrés Escobar was gazing away into the massed and odorous grey-blue mignonette. "Go away before I get angry with you;

you are more Spanish than any Mendoza. The mantón you'll find at home tonight."

He was, frankly, worried about Andrés; not fundamentally—Andrés' loyalty was beyond any personal betrayal—but because he was aware of the essential inflammability of all tropical emotion. The other might get into a rage with Pilar, who never, herself, could fall into such an error, and pay the penalty exacted by a swift gesture toward the hem of her skirt. Then he recalled, still with a slight shudder of delight, the soft dragging feel of her fingers on his cheek. He tied the shawl up sombrely, oppressed by the conviction of mischance he had expressed to Andrés, and despatched it.

Pilar de Lima might, possibly, depart for Peru earlier even than she hoped; boats left not infrequently for Mexico and South America—the Argentine for which La Clavel had longed—and she was welcome to try her mysterious arts upon the seas away from Cuba and Andrés. A sugar bag could easily, at the appropriate moment, be slipped over her head, and a bateau carry her out, with a sum of gold, at night to a departing ship. There would be no trouble, after she had been seen, in getting her on board. And Charles Abbott thought of her, in her silent whiteness, corrupting one by one the officers and crew; a vague hatred would spread over the deck, forward and aft; and through the cabins, the hearts, her suggestions and breath of evil touched. They would never see Mexico, he decided; but, on a calm purple night in the Gulf, a sanguine and volcanic inferno of blackened passion would burst around the flicker of her blanched dress and face no colder in death than in life.

*

*   *

Charles Abbott's thoughts returned continually to Andrés; in the shadowy region of his brain the latter was like a vividly and singly illuminated figure. He remembered, too, the occasion of his first seeing Andrés, at the Hotel Inglaterra: they had gone together into the restaurant, where, over rum punches and cigars, the love he had for him had been born at once. It was curious—that feeling; a thing wholly immaterial, idealizing. He had speculated about it before, but without coming to the end of its possibilities, the bottom of its meaning. There was no need to search for a reason for the love of women; that, it might be, was no more than mechanical, the allurement cast by nature about its automatic purpose. It belonged to earth, where it touched any sky was not

Charles' concern; but his friendship for Andrés Escobar had no relation to material ends.

At first it had been upheld, vitalized, by admiration, qualities perceptible to his mind, to analysis; he had often reviewed them—Andrés' deep sense of honor, his allegiance to a conduct free of self, his generosity, his slightly dramatic but inflexible courage, the fastidious manners of his person. His clothes, the sprig of mimosa he preferred, the angle of his hat and the rake back, through an elbow, of his malacca cane, were all satisfying, distinguished. But Charles' consciousness of these actual traits, details, had vanished before an acceptance of Andrés as a whole, uncritically. What, once, had been a process of thought had become an emotion integral with his own subconscious being.

Something of his essential character had entered Andrés, and a part of Andrés had become bound into him. This, as soon as she had grown into the slightest menace to it, had cast Pilar de Lima from his consideration. It had been no effort, at the moment necessary he had forgotten her; just as Andrés, faced with the truth, would put her away from him. The bond between them, Charles told himself, was forged from pure gold.

This was running through his head on the

night of the danzón. He was seated at the entrance of the United States Club, where the sharp Yankee accents of the gamblers within floated out and were lost in the narrow walled darkness of Virtudes Street. It was no more than eleven, the Tacon Theatre would be empty yet. . . . Charles had no intention of going to the danzón, but at the same time he was the victim of a restless curiosity in connection with it; he had an uncomfortable oppression at the vision of Andrés, with Pilar in the bright shawl, on the floor crowded with the especial depravities of Havana.

The Spanish officers had made it customary for men of gentility to go into the criolla festivities; they were always present, the young and careless, the drunken and degenerate; and that, too, added to Charles' indefinable sense of possible disaster. In a way, it might be an excellent thing for him to attend, to watch, the danzón. If Andrés were infatuated he would be blind to the dangers, both the political and those emanating from the mixture of bloods. At this moment the game inside ended, and a knot of men, sliding into their coats, awkwardly grasping broad-brimmed hats, appeared, departing for the Tacon Theatre. A perfunctory nodded invitation for him to accompany them settled the indecision in Charles Abbott's mind. And, a half hour later, he was seated in a palco of the second tier, above the dance.

Familiar with them, he paid no attention to the sheer fantastic spectacle; the two orchestras, one taking up the burden of sound when the other paused, produced not for him their rasping dislocated rhythm. He was aware only of floating skirts, masks and dark or light faces, cigars held seriously in serious mouths. Charles soon saw that Andrés and Pilar de Lima had not yet arrived. As he leaned forward over the railing of the box, Gaspar Arco de Vaca, sardonic and observing, glanced up and saluted with his exaggerated courtesy. He disappeared, there was a knock at the closed door behind Charles, and de Vaca entered.

There was a general standing acknowledgement of his appearance; the visor of his dress cap was touched for every man present, and he took a vacated chair at Charles' side. "You weren't attracted to my white absinthe," he said easily. On the contrary, Charles replied, he had liked Pilar very well, although she had annoyed him by foolish tales of a Spanish interest in him.

"She is, of course, an agent," de Vaca admitted indifferently. "We almost have to keep her in a cage, like a leopard from Tartary. She has killed three officers of high rank; although we do not prefer her as an assassin. She is valuable as a drop of acid, here, there; and extraordinary individuals often rave about her. We'll have to garrotte her some time, and that will be a pity."

There was a flash of color below, of carmine and golden orange, and Charles recognized Pilar wrapped, from her narrow shoulders to her delicate ankles, in the mantón. Andrés Escobar, with a protruding lip and sullen eyes, was at her side. Suddenly de Vaca utterly astounded Charles; with a warning pressure of his hand he spoke at the younger man's ear:

"I am leaving at once for Madrid, a promotion has fortunately lifted me from this stinking black intrigue, and I have a memory . . . from the sala de Armas, the echo of a sufficiently spirited compliment. As I say, I am off; what is necessary to you is necessary—a death in Havana or a long life at home. Where I am concerned you have bought your right to either. You cannot swing the balance against Spain. And I have this for you to consider. Your friend, Escobar, has reached the end of his journey. It will accomplish nothing to inform him; he is not to walk from the theatre. Very well— if you wish to hatch your seditious wren's eggs tomorrow, if you wish to wake tomorrow at all, stay away from him. Anything else will do no good except, perhaps, for us."

Charles Abbott sat with a mechanical gaze on the floor covered with revolving figures. He realized instantly that Gaspar Arco de Vaca had been truthful. The evidence of that lay in the logic of his words, the ring of his voice. The officer rose, saluted, and left. Andrés had come to the end of his journey! It was incredible. He had not moved from the spot where Charles had first seen him; he had taken off his hat, and his dark faultlessly brushed hair held in a smooth gleam the reflection of a light.

Andrés turned with a chivalrous gesture to Pilar, who, ignoring it completely, watched with inscrutable eyes the passing men. The shawl, on her, had lost its beauty; it was malevolent, screaming in color; contrasted with it her face was marble. How, Charles speculated desperately, was Andrés to be killed? And then he saw. A tall young Spaniard with a jeering countenance, in the uniform of a captain in a regiment not attached at Havana, stopped squarely, with absolute impropriety, before Pilar and asked her to dance. Andrés Escobar, for the moment, was too amazed for objection; and, as Pilar was borne away, he made a gesture of denial that was too late.

He glanced around, as though to see if anyone had observed his humiliation; and Charles Abbott instinctively drew back into the box. As he did this he cursed himself with an utter loathing. Every natural feeling impelled him below, to go blindly to the support of Andrés. There must be some way—a quick shifting of masks and escape through a side door—to get him safely out of the hands of Spain. This, of course, would involve, endanger, himself, but he would welcome the necessity of that acceptance. Gaspar de Vaca had indicated the price he might well pay for such a course—the end, at the same time, of himself; not only the death of his body but the ruin of his hopes and high plans. Nothing, he had told himself a thousand times, should be allowed to assail them. Indeed, he had discussed just such a contingency as this with Andrés. Theoretically there had been no question of the propriety of an utter seeming selfishness; the way, across a restaurant table, had been clear.

THE BRIGHT SHAWL

*

*   *

In the box the other Americans maintained a steady absorbed commenting on the whirling color of the danzón. One, finally, attracted by the mantón on Pilar de Lima, called the attention of the others to her Chinese characteristics. They all leaned forward, engaged by the total pallor of her immobility above the blazing silk. They exclaimed when she left the Spanish officer and resumed her place by Andrés Escobar's side. "Isn't that peculiar?" Charles was asked. "You are supposed to know all about these dark affairs. Isn't it understood that the women keep to their own men? And that Cuban, Abbott, you know him; we often used to see you with him!"

"Yes," Charles Abbott acknowledged, "partners seldom leave each other. That is Andrés Escobar.'

He paid no more heed to the voices about him, but sat with his gaze, his hopes and fears, fastened on Andrés and Pilar. Back again, she was, as usual, silent, dragging her fingers through the knotted magenta fringe of the shawl. Andrés, though, was speaking in short tense phrases that alternated with concentrated angry pauses. She lifted her arms to him, and they began to

[207]

dance. They remained, however, characteristic of the danzón, where they were, turning slowly and reversing in a remarkably small space. They were a notably graceful couple, and they varied, with an intricate stepping, the general monotony of the measure.

Charles had an insane impulse to call down to Andrés, to attract his attention, and to wave him away from the inimical forces gathering about him. Instead of this he lighted a cigarette, with hands the reverse of steady, and concentrated all his thoughts upon the fact of Cuban independence. That, he told himself, was the only thing of importance in his life, in the world. And it wasn't Cuba alone, but the freedom of life at large, that rested, in part at least, on the foundation he might help to lay, the beginning solidity of human liberty, superiority. He forced himself to gaze with an air of indifference at the dancing below him; but, it seemed, wherever he looked, the mantón floated into his vision. He saw, now, nothing else, neither Pilar nor Andrés, but only the savage challenging fire of silks. The shawl's old familiar significance had been entirely lost—here he hated and feared it, it was synonymous with all that threatened his success. It gathered into its folded and draped square the evil of the danzón, the spoiled mustiness of joined and debased bloods, the license under a grotesque similitude of restraint.

This was obliterated by a wave of affection for Andrés so strong that it had the effect of an intolerable physical pressure within his body: his love had the aspect of a tangible power bound to assert itself or to destroy him. With clenched hands he fought it back, he drove it away before the memory of the other. Voices addressed him, but he paid no attention, the words were mere sounds from a casual sphere with which he had nothing in common. He must succeed in his endeavor, put into actuality at this supreme moment his selfless projection of duty, responsibility. For it was, in spite of his preoccupation with its personal possibilities, an ideal to which he, as an entity, was subordinated. He recalled the increasing number of destinies in which he was involved, that were being thrust upon him, and for which, at best, he would become accountable. So much more lay in the immediate future than was promised—justified—in the present.

Here, too, Andrés was at fault—precisely the accident had happened to him that he was so strict in facing for others. His absorption wouldn't, as an infatuation, continue; or, rather, it could not have lasted . . . long. But already it had been long enough to finish, to kill, Andrés. Charles rose uncontrollably to his feet; he would save his friend from the menace of the whole Spanish army. But de Vaca, whose every accent carried conviction, had been explicit: he particularly would not have spoken under any other circumstance. He had, in reality, been tremendously flattering in depending to such a degree on Charles' coolness and intellect. Gaspar de Vaca would have taken no interest in a sentimentalist. The officer without question had found in Charles Abbott a strain of character, a resolution, which he understood, approved; to a certain extent built on. He had, in effect, concluded that Charles and himself would act similarly in similar positions.

It was, Charles decided, at an end; he must go on as he had begun. A strange numb species of calm settled over him. The vast crowded floor, the boxes on either hand, sweeping tier on tier to the far hidden ceiling, surrounding the immense chandelier glittering with crystal lustres, were all removed, distant, from him. The Tacon Theatre took on the appearance of a limitless pit into which all human life had been poured, ar-

THE BRIGHT SHAWL

bitrarily thrown together, and, in the semblance of masquerading gaiety, made to whirl in a time that had in its measure the rattle of bones, a drumming on skulls. This conception sickened him, he could, he felt, no longer breathe in a closeness which he imagined as fetid; and Charles realized that, at least, there was no need for him to remain. Indeed, it would be better in every way to avoid the impending, the immediate, catastrophe.

With a hasty incoherent remark he secured his hat and left the box. Outside, in the bare corridor, he paused and his lips automatically formed the name Andrés Escobar. In a flash he saw the gathering disintegration of the Escobar family—Vincente dead, his body dishonored; Narcisa, ineffable, flower-like, sacrificed to dull ineptitude; Domingo, who had been so cheerfully round, furrowed with care, his spirit dead before his body; Carmita sorrowing; and Andrés, Andrés the beautiful, the young and proud, betrayed, murdered in a brawl at a negro dance. What disaster! And where, in the power of accomplishment, they had failed, where, fatally, they had been vulnerable, was at their hearts, in their love each for the other, or in the fallibility of such an emotion as Andrés felt for Pilar. He, Charles

[211]

Abbott, must keep free from that entanglement. This reassurance, however, was not new; all the while it had supported him.

He made his way down the broad shallow steps, passing extraordinary figures—men black and twisted like the carvings of roots in the garb of holiday minstrels; women coffee-colored and lovely like Jobaba, their faces pearly with rice powder, in yellow satin or black or raw purple, their feet in high-heeled white kid slippers. Where they stood in his way he brushed them unceremoniously, hastily, aside, and he was followed by low threatening murmurs, witless laughter. A man, loyal to the Cuban cause, attempted to stop him, to repeat something which, he assured Charles, was of grave weight; but he went on heedlessly.

His passage became, against his reasoning mind, a flight; and he cursed, with an unbalanced rage, in a minor frenzy, when he saw that he would have to walk through a greater part of the body of the theatre before he could escape. The dancers had, momentarily, thinned out, and he went directly across the floor. There was a flame before his eye, the illusion of a shifting screen of blood; and he found himself facing Pilar de Lima and Andrés; beyond, the Spanish officer, tall and lank and young, was peering at them with an aggressive spite. Charles turned aside, avoiding the tableau. Then he heard Andrés' exasperated voice ordering the girl to come with him to the promenade. Instead of that her glimmering eyes, with lights like the reflection of polished green stones, evading Andrés, sought and found the officer.

Charles Abbott's legs were paralysed, he was held stationary, as though he were helpless in a dream. His heart pounded and burned, and a great strangling impulse shook him like a flag in the wind. "Andrés!" he cried, "Andrés, let her go, she is nothing! Quickly, before it is too late. Remember—" There was a surging concentration so rapid that Charles saw it as a constricting menace rather than the offensive of a group of men. Pilar stooped, her hand at her knee. Charles threw an arm about Andrés, but he was dragged, struggling, away. She was icy in the hell of the mantón. There was a suspension of breathing, of sound, through which a fragile hand with a knife searched and searched. Then a shocking blow fell on Charles Abbott's head and the Tacon Theatre rocked and collapsed in darkness.

THE BRIGHT SHAWL

*

*   *

The sharp closing of a door brought him, a
man advanced in middle age, abruptly to his feet.
He was confused, and swayed dizzily, with out-
stretched arms as though he were grasping vainly
for the dissolving fragments of a shining mirage
of youth. They left him, forever, and he stood
regaining his strayed sense of immediacy. He
was surprisingly weary, in a gloom made evident
by the indirect illumination of an arc light across
and farther up the street. Fumbling over the
wall he encountered the light switch, and flooded
his small drawing-room with brilliance. The
clock on the mantle, crowned by an eagle with
lifted gilded wings, pointed to the first quarter
past eleven: when he had sunk into his abstraction from the present, wandered back into the
sunlight of Havana and his days of promise, it
had been no more than late afternoon; and now
Mrs. Vauxn and her daughter, his neighbors, had
returned from their dinner engagement. He
wondered, momentarily, why that hour and ceremony had passed unattended for him, and then
recalled that Bruton and his wife, who kept his
house, had gone to the funeral of a relative, leaving on the dining-room table, carefully covered,

some cuts of cold meat, a salad of lettuce, bran bread and fresh butter, and the coffee percolator with its attachment for a plug in the floor.

To the rest, he had faithfully told Mrs. Bruton, who was severe with him, he'd attend. In place of that he had wandered into an amazing memory of his beginning manhood. The beginning, he told himself, and, in many ways the end— since then he had done little or nothing. After the ignominy of his deportation from Cuba—impending satisfactory negotiations between the United States and Spain, he gathered later, had preserved him from the dignity of political martyrdom—a drabness of life had caught him from which he could perceive no escape. Not, he was bound to add, that he had actively looked for one. No, his participation in further events had been interfered with by a doubt, his life had been drawn into an endless question. If he had walked steadily past Andrés Escobar, left him to a murder which, after all, he, Charles Abbott, had been powerless to stop, would he have gone on to the triumph of his ideal?

In addition to this there was the eternal speculation over the relation, in human destiny, of the heart to the head—which, in the end, would, must, triumph? There was no necessity in his final

[215]

philosophy for the optimism, where men are concerned, that had been his first stay. He wasn't so sure now—but was he certain of anything?—of the coming victory of right, of the spreading, from land to land, of freedom. Did life reach upward or down, or was it merely the circling of a carrousel, the whirling of the danzón? Nothing, for him, could be settled, definite. He was inclined to the belief that the blow of the scabbard on his head. . . . That, however, like the rest, was indeterminate. He came back eternally to the same query—had he, as for so long, so wearily, he had insisted to himself, failed, proved weak for the contentions of existence on a positive plane? Had he become a part, a member, of the nameless, the individually impotent, throng? His sympathies were, by birth, aristocratic rather than humane; he preferred strength to acquiescence; but there were times now, perhaps, when he was aging, when there was a relief in sinking into the sea of humility.

Then his thoughts centered again on Howard Gage; who, before leaving that afternoon, had unpleasantly impressed Charles Abbott by his inelasticity, the fixity of his gaze upon the ground. Howard had been involved in a war of a magnitude that swamped every vestige of the long-sustained Cuban struggle. And he admitted his relation to this had been one of bitter necessity:

"I had to go, we all did," Howard Gage had said. "There wasn't any music about it, any romance. It had to be done, that was all, and it was. Don't expect me to be poetic."

Yes, the youth of today were, to Charles' way of thinking, badly off. Anyone who could not be poetic, who wouldn't be if he had the chance, was unfortunate, limited, cramped. Visions, ideals, were indispensable for youth. Why, damn it, love was dependent on dreams, unreality. He had never known it; but he was able to appreciate what it might be in a man's life. He no longer scorned love, or the woman he was able to imagine—a tender loveliness never out of a slightly formal beauty. For her the service parts of the house would have no existence; and, strangely, he gave no consideration to children.

It wasn't that he minded loneliness; that was not an unmixed evil, especially for a man whose existence was chiefly spun from memories, speculations, and conditioned by the knowledge that he had had the best of life, its fullest measure, at the beginning. He had never again seen a woman like La Clavel, a friend who could compare with Andrés, wickedness such as Pilar's, days and players as brilliant as those of Havana before, well—before he had passed fifty. If the trade winds still blew, tempering the magnificence of the Cuban nights, they no longer blew for him. But Havana, as well, had changed.

The piano next door took up, where it had been dropped, the jota from Liszt's Rhapsody Espagnol. It rippled and sang for a moment and then ended definitely for the night. Other dancers, Charles reasonably supposed, continued the passionate art of that lyric passage; he read of them, coming from Spain to the United States for no other purpose. He had no doubt about their capability, and no wish to see them. They would do for Howard Gage. What if he, instead of Charles Abbott, had been at the Tacon Theatre the night Andrés had died? That was an interesting variation of the old question—what, in his predicament, would Howard Gage have done? Walked away, probably, holding his purpose undamaged! But Andrés could never have loved Howard Gage; Andrés, for his attachment, required warmth, intensity, the ornamental forms of honor; poetry, briefly. That lost romantic time, that day in immaculate white linen with a spray of mimosa in its button-hole!

There were some flowers, Charles recalled,

[218]

THE BRIGHT SHAWL

standing on the table in the hall, dahlias; and he walked out and drew one into the lapel of his coat. It was without scent, just as, now, life was unscented; yet, surveying himself in the mirror over the vase, he saw that the sombreness of his attire was lightened by the spot of red. Nothing, though, could give vividness to his countenance, that was dry and dull, scored with lines that resembled traces of dust. The moustache across his upper lip was faded and brittle. It was of no account; if he had lacked ultimately the courage, the stamina, to face and command life, he was serene at the threat of death.

Suddenly hungry, he went into the dining-room and removed the napkins, turned the electricity into the percolator. Then, with a key from under the edge of the cloth on a console-table, he opened a door of the sideboard, and produced a tall dark bottle of Marquis de Riscal wine, and methodically drew the cork. Charles Abbott wiped the glass throat and, seated, poured out a goblet full of the translucent crimson liquid. It brought a slight flush to his cheeks, a light in his eyes, and the shadow of a vital humor, a past challenge, to his lips. He had lifted many toasts in that vintage, his glass striking with a clear vibration against other eagerly held glasses.

More often than not they—Tirso, the guardsman
in statue, Remigio, Jaime, Andrés and himself—
had drunk to La Clavel. He drank to her, probably the sole repository of her memory, her splendor, on earth, now. "La Clavel," he said her
name aloud. And then, "Andrés."

A sharp gladness seized him that Andrés had,
almost at the last, heard his voice, his shouted
warning and apprehension and love. If liberty,
justice, were to come, one life, two, could make
no difference; a hundred years, a hundred hundred, were small measures of time. And if all
were doomed, impossible, open to the knife of a
fateful Pilar, why, then, they had had their companionship, their warmth, a period of unalloyed
fidelity to a need that broke ideals like reeds.
Perhaps what they had found was, after all,
within them, that for which they had swept the
sky.

THE END